THE DEADLY

JOHN FRANKLIN BARDIN was born in Cincinnati in 1916. After a difficult childhood – including the loss of his mother through mental illness – he lived in Chicago and New York, where he was an executive of an advertising agency. He published ten novels and taught creative writing as well as advertising. Bardin died in the East Village on 9 July, 1981.

By the same author

The Last of Philip Banter
Devil Take the Blue-Tailed Fly

THE DEADLY
PERCHERON

John Franklin Bardin

A big thank you from the publishers to Lizzie Francke for
introducing us to the weird and wonderful world of John
Franklin Bardin. We also recommend that you watch *Mona Lisa*
again once you've read the novel

First published in the UK in 1947 by Victor Gollancz

This edition published in Great Britain in 2000 by
Canongate Crime, an imprint of
Canongate Books Ltd, 14 High Street,
Edinburgh EH1 1TE

10 9 8 7 6 5 4 3 2 1

British Library Cataloguing-in-Publication Data
A catalogue record for this book is available on
request from the British Library

ISBN 1 84195 013 0

Typeset by Palimpsest Book Production Limited,
Polmont, Stirlingshire
Printed and bound in Great Britain by
Omnia Books Limited, Glasgow

To
My Wife, Rhea

CONTENTS

1 Easy Money 1
2 Gift Horse 17
3 A Question of Motivation 33
4 Non Compos Mentis 45
5 In Which a Man Runs Down 61
6 Between Two Worlds 79
7 The Dilemma 95
8 Memory of Pain 111
9 Memory of Pain II 129
10 Total Recall 141
11 The Beginning of the End 155
12 Percherons Don't Come Cheap 165
13 A Knife Stained Darkly 181
Epilogue 199

EASY MONEY

Jacob Blunt was my last patient. He came into my office wearing a scarlet hibiscus in his curly blond hair. He sat down in the easy chair across from my desk, and said, 'Doctor, I think I'm losing my mind.'

He was a handsome young man and apparently a healthy one. There were certainly no surface manifestations of neuroses. He did not seem nervous – nor did he seem to be suppressing a tendency to be nervous – his blue eyes were steady, his suit neat. The features of his face were strong, his shoulders were nicely made and except for a slight limp he carried himself well. I would not have believed he belonged in my consultation room if it hadn't been for the outrageous flower in his hair.

'Most of us have similar apprehensions at some time or other,' I said. 'During an emotional crisis, or after periods of sustained overwork, I, too, have been uncertain of my sanity.'

'Crazy people see things, don't they?' he asked. 'Things that really aren't there?' He leaned forward as if he were afraid he might miss my answer if he did not get closer to me.

'Hallucinations are a common symptom of mental disorder,' I agreed.

'And when you don't only see things – but things happen to you – crazy things, I mean – that's having hallucinations, isn't it?'

'Yes,' I said, 'a person who is mentally ill often lives in a world of his own imagining, an unreal world. He withdraws completely from reality.'

Jacob leaned back and sighed happily. 'That's me!' he said. 'I am nuts, thank God! It isn't really happening!'

He seemed wholly at ease. His face had relaxed into a crooked grin that was rather nice. My information had obviously relieved him. This was unusual; I had never before met a neurotic who admitted wanting to lose his mind. Nor had I seen one who felt happy about it.

'That's a pretty flower you have in your hair,' I said. 'Tropical, isn't it?' I had to begin somewhere to find out what was wrong with him, and the flower was the only unnatural thing I could find.

He fingered it. 'Yeah,' he said, 'it's a hibiscus. I had a devil of a time getting it, too! Had to run all over town this morning before I found a place that had one!'

'Are you so fond of them?' I asked. 'Why not a rose or a gardenia? They're cheaper, and surely easier to buy.'

He shook his head. 'Nope. I've worn them at times, but it had to be a hibiscus today. Joe said it had to be a hibiscus today.'

It began to look as if he might be insane. His conversation seemed incoherent and he was entirely too happy about the whole affair. I began to be interested.

'Who is Joe?' I asked.

Blunt had taken a cigarette out of the box on my desk and was now fumbling with the lighter. He looked up in surprise. 'Joe? Oh, he's one of my little men. The one in the purple suit. He gives me ten dollars a day for

2

wearing a flower in my hair. Only he picks the flowers and that's where it gets tough! He can pick the screwiest flowers!'

He gave me some more of that crooked grin. It was almost as if he were saying 'I know this sounds silly, but it's the way my mind works. I can't really help it.'

'Joe is only the one who gives you flowers, is that right?' I asked him. 'There are others?'

'Oh, sure there are others. I do things for a lot of little guys, that's what has me worried! Only you're mixed up about Joe. He doesn't give me the flowers. I have to go out and buy them myself. He only pays me for wearing them.'

'You say that there are other "little guys" – who are they and what do they do?'

'Oh, there's Harry,' he said. 'He's the one who wears green suits and pays me to whistle at Carnegie Hall. And there's Eustace – he wears tattersall waistcoats and pays me to give quarters away.'

'Your quarters?'

'No, his. He gives me twenty quarters every day. I get another ten dollars for giving them away.'

'Why not keep them?'

He frowned. 'Oh, no! I couldn't do that! I wouldn't get the ten dollars if I kept them. Eustace only pays me when I succeed in giving them all away.'

He reached into his pocket and pulled out a handful of shiny new quarters. 'That reminds me,' he said. 'I'm meeting Eustace at six, and I have all these to give away yet. Take one of them, will you please?'

And he flipped a quarter on to my desk. I picked it up and put it in my pocket. I did not want to antagonize him.

He watched me closely. 'It's real, isn't it?' he asked.

'Yes,' I said. 'It was real.'

'Do me a favour. Bite it.'

'No,' I said. 'I don't have to bite it. I know a genuine coin when I see one.'

'Go ahead and bite it,' he said. 'So you know it isn't counterfeit.'

I took the quarter out of my pocket, placed it in my mouth and bit it. I wanted to humour him. 'It's real enough,' I said.

His grin sagged, then disappeared. 'That's what worries me,' he said.

'What?'

'If I'm crazy, doc, then you can cure me. But if I'm not crazy, and these little men are real, why then there are such things as leprechauns and they are giving away a tremendous treasure – and then we'd all have to begin to believe in fairies, and there's simply no telling where that would lead to!'

At that point I thought I was on the verge of uncovering his neuroses. He seemed very excited, almost frantic – and he had thrown a great deal of new information at me suddenly. I decided to ignore his reference to 'leprechauns' and 'fairies' for the time being, while continuing to question him about the one tangible piece of evidence: the quarter.

'What has this to do with Eustace and the quarters?' I asked him.

'Can't you see, doc? If I'm crazy – if I just imagine Eustace – what about the quarters? They're real enough, aren't they?'

'Perhaps they belong to you,' I suggested. 'Couldn't you have gone to your bank and withdrawn them, and then forgotten about it?'

He shook his head. 'Nope. It's not that easy. I haven't been to my bank in months.'

'Why not?'

'Don't have to. Why go to the bank and draw money if you're making thirty to forty dollars a day? I haven't spent any of my own money since last Christmas.'

'Since last Christmas?'

'Yeah. I met Joe on Christmas day. In an Automat. He didn't know how to get coffee out of the gadget there, and I showed him. We fell to talking and he asked me if I wanted to make some easy money. I said, "Sure, why not?" I didn't know then what a silly job it would turn out to be. But I was bored with the job I had – I was clerking in a haberdashery – and anxious to do something more interesting. I really don't have to work, you know. I have a steady income from a trust fund. But the trustee is a cranky old guy who always lectures me about the virtues of having a job. He says, "Doing a task well builds character."

'I started to work for Joe that very day and after a couple of weeks I met Eustace and then Harry through Joe. Joe was pleased with my work. He said I was trustworthy. He said the little men always had trouble finding guys they could trust.'

I was fascinated. This promised to be one of the more curious cases of my career. Most abnormalities adhere closely to a few, well-established patterns. It is not often that you find a man so imaginatively insane as Jacob Blunt seemed to be.

'Tell me, Mr Blunt,' I asked, 'just what exactly is your trouble? It seems to me that you lead an excellent life – you certainly make enough money. What is the matter?'

Once again I saw him discomfited. He looked away from me, and his grin came and went before he answered.

'There's nothing wrong, I guess,' he said. 'That is, if you're sure that Joe and Harry and Eustace are hallucinations?'

5

'That is what I would say they probably are.'

He smiled again. 'Well, if you're right, I'm just nuts and that's fine. But what worries me is the dough! If those quarters are real, how can Eustace be imaginary?'

'Perhaps, as I suggested before, you get them from your bank, and then forget you have made a withdrawal.'

His smile broadened. He reached into his breast-pocket and pulled out his bankbook. He handed it across the desk to me. 'What about this then, doc?' he asked.

I looked at the figures in the book. There had been regular, quarterly deposits of a thousand dollars each for the past two years, but there had not been a withdrawal since the 20th December, 1942. I handed the bankbook back to him.

'I tell you I haven't been to the bank since before last Christmas,' he repeated.

'What about the deposits?' I asked.

'My trustee makes those,' he said. 'From my father's estate. It's in trust until I'm twenty-five.'

I thought for a moment. If I could only get him to give me a coherent account of what had been happening to him, I might be able to inquire a little more deeply into the nature of his trouble. 'Suppose you go back to the beginning and tell me all about it,' I proposed.

He looked steadily at me, and his look made me feel uncomfortable. I had an idea that he knew how puzzled I was, and that my confusion disturbed him.

'It's as I told you,' he said. 'I met Joe in the Automat. He said he'd give me a trial at flower-wearing and, if I was good at it, I could do it regular. He was so pleased with what he called my "earnestness" that he recommended me to Harry and Eustace. I've been whistling

6

for Harry and giving quarters away for Eustace ever since . . .'

This was getting us no place. Absurd as his fantasies were, they were consistent. 'What do you do for Harry? Did you say whistle?' I asked wearily.

'Sure. At Carnegie Hall. At Town Hall. Sometimes in the balcony. Sometimes downstairs. I don't have to do it loud, and I may sit off by myself so I don't annoy anybody. It's a lot of fun. Last night I whistled "Pistol-Packin' Mama" all through Beethoven's "Eighth". You oughtta try it some time! It does you good!'

I smothered a smile. I had begun to like the boy, and I did not want him to think I was laughing at him.

'These "little men" – why did you say they hire you to do all these peculiar things?'

He reached for another cigarette and fumbled again with my lighter. Most of my patients smoke – I encourage them to because it makes them feel at ease – and it gives me an opportunity to watch their reactions to a petty annoyance if my cigar-lighter is balky. Often a man or woman who is superficially calm will reveal an inner nervousness by getting disproportionately aggravated at the futile spark. But not Jacob Blunt, he spun the tiny wheel patiently and phlegmatically until the unwilling flame appeared. Then he answered me.

'They're leprechauns. Came originally from Ireland, but now they're all over the world. They've had a tremendous treasure for all eternity and until recently they guarded it jealously. Now, for reasons of their own that I can't get Eustace to tell me, they've started to distribute it. Joe says they've got hundreds of men working for them all over the country. Some pretty big men, too, Joe says. People you'd never guess.'

'You mean they are fairies, like gnomes or elves?' Sometimes if you can show a patient the infantile level of his obsession, you can give him a jolt that will start him back on the road to reality. 'Don't tell me you believe in fairies!' I scoffed.

'They're not fairies,' he protested. 'They're little men in green and purple suits. You've probably passed them on the street!'

I was getting nowhere. Soon I would be arguing with my patient on his terms. I had to find a way to change the direction of the conversation. As it was, he was leading it, not I.

'Suppose you aren't mentally ill, Mr Blunt, what then?'

He grew serious. For the first time he seemed sick, anxious.

'That's what has me worried, doc! What if I'm not crazy?'

'Then the "little men" are real,' I said. 'Then there are such things as leprechauns. You don't really believe that, do you?'

He was silent, undecided. Then he shook his head violently. 'No, I won't believe it! It couldn't be! I must be crazy!'

I thought it was about time to reassure him. 'Let me decide that,' I said. 'That's my job. People who suffer from hallucinations such as yours usually defend them rigorously. They never entertain the possibility of a doubt as to the reality of their imagined experiences. But you do. That is encouraging.'

'But what about the money, doc? The quarters? They're real enough, aren't they?'

'Let's not consider that part of it now. Suppose you tell me a little about yourself. Talk to me about your childhood, your youth, your girl – you have a girl, haven't you? – whatever comes first to your mind.'

I was hopelessly confused. Usually a psychiatrist can

see the flaw in the logic of a schizoid's dream world. It is patently an irrational mechanism. The difficulty normally lies in getting the patient to talk about his inner life. Here, however, this was not the case. Jacob seemed eager to confide the details of his 'little men' and their 'easy money' to me; but, besides doing that, he had presented a certain amount of evidence that at least some of his experiences were true, and if this were so he might not be insane. All I could do was to urge him to talk some more, hoping that he would say something that would help me help him.

'What will telling you the story of my life have to do with Eustace and Joe?' he asked.

'Take my word for it that it may have a great deal of bearing on your problem,' I said.

He was reluctant to begin. Nor was he as much at ease as he had been before. He had stopped smiling, and his eyes were dull.

'I'm a Dead-End Kid,' he said, 'who was raised on Park Avenue. You probably know all about my old man, John Blunt. He had more money than was good for him. Just about the time of the First World War he sold his carriage-making business to one of the big automobile companies and from then on he was rolling in dough. He bought himself a seat on the Exchange and kept right on making money until he died of apoplexy a few years back. He left all his dough to me, but he tied it up in a trust so I can't get at it until I'm twenty-five.'

'How old are you now?'

'I'm twenty-three. I've two more years to go. But that isn't what worries me. I've got plenty of dough.'

'Yes,' I said, 'I know.'

'I really was a hell-raiser when I was a kid. I wore out two or three governesses a year. My mother died when I was a brat, that's why I had the governesses.

My old man never paid much attention to me. I used to run wild. I made friends with all sorts of kids. I always had more money than any of the others, and I was so much trouble to have around that none of the servants minded much if I didn't come home for days at a time.'

'How old were you when you started running away from home?'

'Nine or ten.' He dug into his coat pocket and took out his wallet. From it he drew a well-thumbed photograph which he handed to me. 'That's a picture of me at about that time,' he said. 'The kid with me was a friend of mine – the ugliest little shrimp I ever did see. I called him Pruney.'

I looked at the photograph. It was the kind a strolling photographer makes. Jacob looked surprisingly the same – even as a child he had that lopsided grin. But it was the image of his small companion that held my eye. He was a small boy dressed in a dirty sailor's suit, yet his face was uglier than I have ever seen on a child other than a cretin. It was an ugliness you would expect to find in a man of forty or more, not a young boy. And on the back of the photograph were scrawled the initials: E.A.B.

'What do these stand for?' I asked.

Jacob looked at them, shrugged. 'I don't know. I had even forgotten about Pruney and this old picture until – after my old man's death – I was going through his desk one day and found this in a cubbyhole. I guess it meant something to him.'

I stuck the photograph in my pocket. I wanted to see if my patient would resent this act of possession. But he did not seem to notice it. Baffled, I tried another tack: 'Where did you sleep when you were away from home?'

'In hotels. In the Park. I spent a lot of time around Central Park. Sometimes at the houses of friends. I always had a lot of friends.'

'Hardly a normal childhood,' I said. 'Why didn't your father stop you? Didn't he know what you were doing?'

Jacob laughed. He threw back his head and laughed loudly, a harsh, cynical laugh. 'I tell you my old man didn't give a damn,' he said, 'about me, or anybody! He hired people to look after me – why should he bother?'

I said nothing. Jacob stopped laughing. He did not go on. I did not know what to think. He had obviously had an extraordinary life so far, and not a healthy one. I was not surprised that he was neurotic. He had never had a family, no one had ever loved him. Or had there been someone . . . ?

'When did you first fall in love?' I asked. Perhaps, the clue lay there . . .

'When I was fourteen. With the cigarette girl at the St Moritz. She was a blonde and she had nice legs. I remember I bought her a black silk nightgown for Christmas. Did you ever buy a girl a black silk nightgown?'

His grin was contagious. 'Why, yes, I suppose so,' I said.

'Who?'

'My wife, I guess.'

'Oh.' He was disappointed. Then he said, 'Well, I suppose we all do that at one time or another.'

'But not at fourteen. That's a rather tender age, don't you think?'

He smiled deprecatingly. 'You don't understand, doc. At fourteen I'd been around. I'd been underfoot in New York hotels since I was knee-high. I knew all about cigarette girls and things at fourteen.'

'This cigarette girl was your first love, you say? How many times have you been in love since then?'

He started to count up on his fingers, then stopped and shook his head in mock dismay. 'Hundreds of times, I guess,' he said. 'Dozens of times between then and when I went to college. At least a score of times at Dartmouth. I don't know how many times since . . . I'm in love with a redhead right now! I'd marry her if I wasn't crazy!'

'Don't you think you fall into and out of love too easily?' I asked. 'Would you agree that you were emotionally unstable?'

'No, I wouldn't!' He was emphatic. 'I'm just lucky. I've enough money and enough looks to get a woman easily, so it's only natural that I do. What's more normal than falling in love?'

'That's normal enough,' I admitted, 'but what about falling out of it? Most men eventually settle down and get married.'

'Most men don't have the money I have,' he said blithely. And then more seriously, 'And most men don't see little men in green and purple suits!'

Jacob was quiet. During his account of his early life, I was again impressed by his sanity. Except for the 'little men' – and the scarlet hibiscus in his curly blond hair – I had seldom met a more normal young man. For example, a neurotic, when invited to talk about himself and his childhood, is likely to respond in one of two ways: he may either tell a long rambling story in excessive detail that reveals a score of hidden fears and resentments, or he may shut up and refuse to talk. But Jacob had done neither. His response had been of the kind I might have made myself if I should ever have had to answer an over-inquisitive interrogator in this way. He had told a simple, brief, cogent – and, so far as

I could tell, truthful – story in a casual, friendly fashion. The only induction I could make about his character that was in any way profitable from a psychiatric point of view was the fact that he hated his father. I could hardly call this abnormal. From what I knew of him, I wouldn't have liked old John Blunt either. He was the last of the Robber Barons.

On the other hand, some of Jacob's actions were quite peculiar. How had he allowed himself to be inveigled into all this ridiculous business of wearing flowers in his hair, giving quarters away, whistling at Carnegie Hall? I could think of only one probable reason why an otherwise apparently rational young man would do what Jacob had done: he did it because he liked doing it. Hadn't there been a gleam in his eye when he urged me to try whistling a popular tune the next time I attended a concert? Hadn't he said, 'You oughtta try it some time. It does you good!'? And from the way he kept patting at the hibiscus in his hair, I surmised that he enjoyed wearing it. His own account of his past history might supply the cause for the pleasure he took in such outrageous, non-conforming behaviour. He had never had a normal home life; he had no respect for authority, and he enjoyed revolt. His whole personality might be built on this latent need to protest. Being an impulsive, extraverted youth, his protest took the form of tomfoolery and thoughtless waggishness. So he fell in with the suggestions of his 'little men' and liked doing what they told him to do . . . up to a point. Yet the trouble with this seemingly reasonable explanation was that it took for granted the existence of the 'little men'. And I was not ready to take that much for granted.

So I found myself again at a loss. Each time before that I had attempted to analyse my patient's complaint,

I had ended up facing a blank, but quite sane, wall of defence. Now I hesitated to try again.

It was Jacob who made the suggestion. 'Look, doc,' he said, 'we're getting no place fast!' He checked his wrist watch. 'And it's five o'clock already – I'm supposed to meet Eustace at a bar on Third Avenue at six. Why don't you come back to my place while I shave and change my clothes, and we can both go over to the bar and meet Eustace? Then you can see for yourself!'

I looked at him. His eyes were begging me to say yes. Unorthodox as it was I had the feeling that what he suggested was the correct way for me to approach his case, especially if he were neurotic. It showed him that I had confidence in his 'earnestness', and if he felt I trusted him, he might come eventually to trust me – it might be a means of accomplishing a transference. Of course, I knew that there was no Eustace, and I had an idea that all we would do at the bar would be to have a few drinks. But it was worth trying.

'I think that's an excellent idea, Mr Blunt,' I said. 'I should like to meet your friend.'

'Maybe you'd like to go to work for him, too?' he asked. I could not tell whether he was poking fun at me or not.

I laughed and said, 'I might at that. I could use a little extra cash as well as the next one!'

I told Miss Henry, my nurse, that I was leaving for the day and asked her to phone my wife at my home in New Jersey to tell her that I would be late and not to keep dinner for me. I also asked Miss Henry at what time was my first appointment the next day. And then I followed Jacob out of my office into the corridor.

He was still wearing that ridiculous flower in his

hair. If I have an outstanding fault, it is that I am rather vain about my personal appearance. I have regular features and a sober expression. I am perhaps a little too fastidious, although I don't think I am conceited. Still, when I go out with others, I expect them to be similarly neat and tidy. I disliked having to walk the streets with a man who wore an absurd flower in his hair. While we were waiting for the elevator, I asked him to take it off.

'Oh, I couldn't do that,' he said. 'Eustace would notice it! He might tell Joe and then Joe wouldn't want to hire me again. I have to wear it all day to earn the ten dollars.'

'But can't you take it off now, and put it in your pocket until we're about to meet Eustace? You could put it back on then and he would never be any the wiser.'

'Oh, no! I couldn't do that. That would be dishonest! You forget that the reason the leprechauns hire me all the time to distribute their money is because I'm so trustworthy! I could never betray their trust.'

'I see,' I said. There was nothing to be gained by arguing with him.

Jacob gave me a sidewise look. 'Would you feel better if you had one, too?' he asked. 'The florist I finally found this one at this morning had another one, and his shop is quite near here. They might still have it. If you want, I think we might have time to stop by there so you could have one, too!'

'No, thanks,' I said.

'But it might be a good idea!' he insisted. 'If Eustace saw you voluntarily wearing a flower in your hair, he might tell Joe about it and it might help you to get into Joe's good graces. You might be able to work for Joe as well as Eustace!'

'No, thanks,' I said. 'I can do without a hibiscus right now.'

I was glad the elevator came just then, interrupting the conversation. Sometimes a psychiatrist's life is a hard one.

GIFT HORSE

Jacob gave away all his quarters before I managed to get him into a taxi. It was quite embarrassing. He gave one to the elevator operator, another to the starter, one to a lady in mink who was coming out of the revolving door as we were going in, one to a coloured shoeshine boy who has a stand outside my office building and the last to the doorman. I felt better when we were finally inside the taxi and Jacob had given the driver an address on West Fifty-third Street. I hadn't liked the look the lady in mink had tossed at us as she regarded first the shiny new quarter in her hand, and then the scarlet flower in my patient's hair.

He told me more about himself during the slow ride through rush-hour streets to his apartment. He had graduated from Dartmouth in 1940. The Army hadn't taken him because of an old knee injury sustained in a basketball game during his sophomore year. He was only twenty-one when he finished college because he entered at seventeen, having skipped a grade in child-hood. He said he liked Bach and Mozart and Brahms, redheads and Hemingway. His present redhead was in the chorus of *Nevada!* – he had met her one night when he went backstage. She was, in his words, 'some mouse!'

The taxi stopped in the middle of the block between Fifth and Sixth Avenues on West Fifty-third, and we entered a very modern apartment building. The desk clerk nodded to Jacob, and the elevator operator smiled and called him 'Mr Blunt'. Apparently these people who saw him all the time knew and liked him. If they had thought him queer, they would have treated him differently. Things were certainly not getting any simpler.

I liked his apartment. It was one extraordinarily large room, a small bedroom, a kitchen and a bath. The walls of the main room were a deep blue, one was lined with bookcases; there was a phonograph with ample record shelves and a fireplace with a good Miro hanging above it. The redhead was on the long divan in the centre of the room, half-lying, half-sitting against a striped pillow. Her hair was long, loose, in lovely disarray. Another girl sat more stiffly beside her – a small, neat, childlike creature with soft-brown curls and an open, innocent look in her blue eyes. The redhead glanced up at us as we came into the room, her eyes intense green blurs in her beautiful, blank face.

'Hello, Jakey,' she said in a low, purring voice. 'Denise and I were shopping and we dropped by a minute ago to mix ourselves a drink. Who's your friend?' Both girls were looking at me with unashamed curiosity.

Jacob had stopped smiling, and all his casual friendliness had disappeared. He seemed both startled and displeased to find that there was someone in his apartment. Not that this showed in anything he said. It was only that he was suddenly stiff and wary, even, perhaps, suspicious.

'Dr George Matthews, Nan Bulkely, Denise Hanover,' he mumbled. From the vague wave of his hand, I took it that the tall girl with the blank stare was Nan, the brunette was Denise. Jacob nodded in Nan's direction and said in a slightly louder voice, 'She'll give you a drink if you want it. I'm going in to shave and dress.' And he went out of the room without saying another word.

I walked over and sat down in a chair across from the divan. Nan uncrossed her legs – they were delightful legs, long and well-proportioned, a dancer's legs without a dancer's unsightly muscles. Denise picked up her cocktail and began to sip it, and her eyes studied the glass. But Nan never took her own remarkable eyes off mine. These were as green as a cat's in the dark, but wide and open, disarmingly frank. Yet, except for her eyes, Nan's face was expressionless, empty. Even when she smiled it was like having a full-colour advertisement come to life and smile at you – something out of *Harper's Bazaar* or the *New Yorker*.

'I'm sorry,' she said. 'I didn't catch your name? Jacob mumbles so.'

'I'm George Matthews,' I said.

She opened her eyes a little wider. 'Didn't I hear Jacob say "Doctor"? Or were my ears playing tricks on me?'

'I am a doctor,' I said. 'A psychiatrist.' I did not like Nan at all. She made me feel as though I was a child being pumped by an adult. I looked at the other girl and, as I did, she stood up and walked out of the big room into the kitchen. It was as if some signal had been passed between the two women. This I resented, as well as Nan's questioning. But I was careful not to let her see my resentment – she might tell me something about my patient that would turn out to be valuable. So I answered her questions.

'Are you and Jacob old friends?' was the next one.

'No. As a matter of fact, I saw him for the first time this afternoon in my office. He is my patient.'

She was surprised. I saw her throat tighten and her shoulders grow a little more rigid, although on the whole she controlled herself well. If I hadn't been a trained observer of the subtle psychological reactions that betray a person's emotions, I would not have known how much my simple statement of fact had shocked her.

She was quiet for a moment, and then she asked, 'Did Jacob come to see you of his own free will?'

'So far as I know. Why do you ask?'

'I just never thought he would, that's all,' she said. 'I'm rather glad he has consulted you. I've been awfully worried about the way he's been acting these past few months, but I knew I could never suggest that he visit a psychiatrist. He wouldn't have listened to me.'

It was a clever act. When she asked me if Jacob visited me on his own impulse, I felt that she actually wanted to know – in fact, there was an urgency about the way she asked the question that made me think she had to know. But the reason she gave me for asking me that question was a contrived excuse. I could not help but wonder why she was so concerned over Jacob's having come to see me.

'What has Jacob been doing lately that has you so worried?' I asked her.

'You saw the flower he was wearing, didn't you? In his hair! He says that a friend of his pays him to do that! And it has to be a different flower each day!'

'Have you ever met this friend?'

She regarded me steadily as if she meant to confide in me. 'No, that's the strange thing about it. He has described them to me – there are several of them you know – not one – several "little men" – he's told me all about them, even told me their names, but I have never met one of them. I think they exist only in his imagination.'

'Has he ever shown signs of queerness before, Miss Bulkely?'

She shook her head, her red hair swirling about her shoulders. 'Of course, I haven't known him long – only since last year. But when I first met him he seemed altogether normal.'

I stood up and went over to the mantel to get a closer look at the Miro. I've always liked Miro. There's something marvellously fluid and liquescent about his work, something soothing like a fountain plashing in the evening's distance. But this time I paid little attention to the Miro. I went over to it for the effect, so Nan would not see how important I considered our conversation.

'Would you say he was abnormal now, Miss Bulkely?' I asked.

She stood up too, and walked over to where I was standing. She was tall, slender without being angular, high-breasted. I liked to look at her, but when I looked at her it was difficult to keep my mind on what she was saying. 'Yes, doctor, I would. I've almost decided that Jacob is losing his mind.'

'That is what he thinks himself,' I said. 'I'm not so sure.'

She was standing close to me, her eyes level with mine. 'Doctor, do you think he might get violent?'

I reached into my breast pocket for my cigarettes. That is the pocket where I keep my cards. As I pulled out my cigarette case, my card folder fell onto the floor. Nan stooped immediately to pick it up – stooped quicker than I did myself – then held it in her hand, looking at it. She tore the top card off and held it to her mouth, smiling.

'Do you mind if I take this, doctor? I see it has both your telephone numbers on it. If I have it, I can get you at any time of the day or night if anything should go wrong with Jacob . . .'

What could I say but, 'Yes, of course. Keep it if you wish'? It was as if she had picked my pocket – I had the definite impression that it was my telephone number that she had been after all along – but I would have been foolish to protest. After all, there was no good reason why she should not call me up.

I started to say, 'I have only seen Jacob for an hour or so this afternoon and I am not thoroughly acquainted with his symptoms, but I see no cause for alarm as yet—' when I became aware of the fact that someone, not Nan, had coughed. I turned around to see the other girl, Denise, standing behind us. Her face was flushed and her eyes were round and glistened. She seemed to be making an effort to communicate something to her friend, trying to speak without speaking. Then, I became aware of Jacob's presence at the same moment Nan herself did. He was standing in the doorway that led to the bath; he had changed into a dinner suit and his curly hair was carefully combed. His face was white with anger.

'What has she been telling you about me, doctor?' he demanded.

Nan rushed over to him, put her arm around him. 'I was just telling him about your friends, Jakey. I didn't say a thing you wouldn't have said yourself.'

He pushed her away from him. 'What are you doing here? Why didn't you tell me you were coming?'

She pretended to pout. That was one thing she could not do well, pout. All she accomplished was a crude parody of the childish expression. 'I only wanted to

22

see you, Jakey. I thought you could have dinner with us before the show.'

'You could have telephoned me if you had wanted to do that. How many times have I told you not to come to my place without calling first? Do you want me to tell my man not to let you in?'

Nan was angry now. She went into the foyer and took her wrap from the closet and flung it about her shoulders. Denise, embarrassed, followed her. Nan stood staring back at Jacob and myself, her eyes bright slits of green fire. But when she spoke, she spoke to me.

'Do you see what I mean, doctor? He's mad – stark, raving mad!'

She even slammed the door on the way out – after holding it until her companion was safely outside. It was a good performance.

'Weren't you a little hard on them?' I asked Jacob as we were standing waiting for the elevator. 'I think Miss Bulkely is really concerned about you. You're concerned about yourself, you know. As for Denise, well, I think she was fairly embarrassed.'

'It wasn't that I minded so much Nan's talking about me behind my back,' he said. 'It's that she has begun to follow me around. Everywhere I go, I see her – or that friend of hers. I feel like she's trying to keep me leashed!'

I could understand his resentment and, at the same time, I could see where Nan might have good reason for acting the way she did. Although I had sensed something wrong in her attitude, I seemed compelled to defend her to Jacob – yet I dared not do so more than I had already. If I were to help him, I would have to induce the belief that I was on his side, right or wrong.

23

The taxi took us to a bar and grill in the Sixties on Third Avenue. This was the usual Third Avenue bar-room with Rheingold neon signs in the windows and sawdust on the tile floor. I noticed, while I was waiting for Jacob to pay the cabby, that a large van had been parked in front of the place – a truck with deep sides and screened windows near the roof of its storage space not unlike an oversize paddy wagon. I wondered at the time what it was there for, but I forgot about it almost immediately.

We went into the bar and ordered a couple of beers. Jacob looked around the smoke-filled room and then said, 'I don't think Eustace is here yet.'

I looked about, too. I don't know what I expected to see, surely not Eustace. There were a few booths along one wall, some tables in the rear – a few of which had been pushed aside to make way for a dart game. Most of the customers were clustered around the players, one of whom seemed to be an excellent shot. As I watched I saw three, clean bull's-eyes thrown into the target, a circle chalked on the wall. Then I looked back at Jacob.

'Tell me,' I asked, 'do you really expect Eustace to come?'

'Oh, he'll be here all right. He's usually a little late. He sleeps a lot and has trouble with his alarm clock.'

Was my patient pulling my leg? If he was, he was keeping a perfectly straight face and making a good show of turning around to look every time someone opened the door. I drank some beer and resumed my interest in the dart game.

It was breaking up. Men were turning away, shaking their heads and emitting low whistles. I saw that the target now contained all of the darts – the bull's-eye being particularly crowded. I peered to see who was the egregious marksman. It turned out to be Eustace.

He was a midget scarcely more than three feet high. He had on a bottle-green velvet jacket, a tattersall waistcoat and mauve broadcloth trousers. He walked jauntily from out of the crowd of normal sized men, a broad grin on his face. Somebody yelled at him 'Where did you learn to throw darts like that?' and, without turning around, he answered, 'Once I was one end of a knife-throwing act in a carnival.' Then he saw Jacob. He came over to the bar and held out a hand to be helped up onto the barstool. When he was seated comfortably, he glowered and said to Jacob in a disproportionately bass voice: 'Who's this mug?'

Jacob waved a hand in my direction. 'This is Dr Matthews, Eustace. He'd like to go to work for you, too.'

Before I could protest, Eustace had turned his back on me. 'Can't use him,' he said to Jacob. 'He's not our type.'

This made me angry. Why couldn't I give money away as well as the next one?

'What's so difficult about giving money away?' I said. My voice was loud. 'I don't see why I couldn't do it!' I still hadn't overcome my surprise at finding Eustace was real, and I had to find some way to express my resentment.

Eustace turned around slowly on his stool and gave me a disdainful look. I began to dislike the little man intensely.

'Money?' said Eustace. 'Who's giving away money?'

'Why, Eustace,' said Jacob, 'haven't I been giving money away for you every day for the past six months?'

'Oh, that! That stopped yesterday,' said Eustace. 'Now you're giving away horses. Percherons.' He turned and whistled at the bartender. 'Hey, Herman,' he called in his deepest voice, 'how about a hooker of that lousy hog-dip you call rye?'

'Horses?' said Jacob.

'Yeah, percherons,' said Eustace. 'The kind they use on beer wagons.'

I had been examining Eustace carefully. I was sure he was only a midget. He had the typical cranium of a dwarf, the compressed features, the dominant forehead, the prematurely wrinkled skin. I pointed a finger at him.

'He's only a midget, Jacob,' I said. 'He's not what you think he is. Someone is playing a joke on you.'

Eustace got very angry. He began to jump up and down on his stool like a kid at the circus. His small face got bright red and then dark purple.

'Midget!' he croaked. 'Who the hell's a midget? I'm a leprechaun. Me father came from County Cork!'

Jacob was exasperated, too. 'Now, look what you've done!' he exclaimed. 'Now you'll never get to work for them!'

I refused to be abashed. 'He's not a leprechaun, Jacob!' I insisted. 'Leprechauns are tiny men only six inches high. He's only a midget pretending to be a leprechaun.'

'You're thinking of Irish leprechauns,' said Jacob. 'Eustace is an American leprechaun. His father came over from Ireland and Eustace was born on this side of the water. Leprechauns, like everything else in America, are bigger and better than anywhere else!'

Eustace had quieted down. He contented himself with delivering a withering glance in my direction that was intended as a *coup de grâce*. Then he ignored me.

'Isn't there some place we can go to talk business in private?' he asked Jacob.

26

'You can talk in front of Dr Matthews,' Jacob replied. 'I've told him about our work.'

The bartender set the hooker of rye down in front of the preposterous little fool. He grabbed it greedily and tossed it down his throat skilfully. Then he gave another scornful look.

'Well, if you've told him the harm's already done,' he said. 'But you really ought to be more careful who you talk to!'

If Jacob Blunt had not been a patient of mine, I would have walked away and never seen him again after that. Still it was plainly my duty to stay and see what this hoax would put him up to next.

'You said I'm not to give quarters away any more,' Jacob was saying. 'You said I was to give away horses. But to whom?'

'That's right,' said Eustace. 'Percherons. The big ones. Tonight you're going to give Frances Raye a percheron.'

'Frances Raye!' I said. 'The star of *Nevada!*? Why, she's the most successful actress on Broadway!'

'That's the one,' said Eustace. 'We leprechauns have decided that it's about time she had a percheron.'

'How am I going to get it to her?' asked Jacob. He was frowning – I could see he was not too pleased with this latest assignment.

'I've got it in a truck outside,' said Eustace. 'I'll drive you over with it, and then you can take it out and tether it, go ring her doorbell and present it to her. You get twenty-five dollars for that instead of ten.'

Jacob was decidedly unhappy. I had not seen his grin in some time. Eustace must have noticed it, too.

'Look,' he said, 'what's eating at you? Here I give you a promotion – take you off of quarters and put you on to percherons – and to look at you I'd think I'd fired you! I don't get it!'

Jacob tried to smile. 'You mean I'm to give away a horse every night to – to somebody like Frances Raye?' he stammered.

Eustace nodded his absurd head waggishly. 'That's right. That is, if you do a good job. It all depends on whether you're cut out for percherons. You may be just a good man on quarters.' Here he paused, significantly, and looked at me. 'Some people can't even give quarters away!' he scoffed.

I did not like Eustace at all.

Jacob regarded me over Eustace's head. 'Did you hear what he said, Dr Matthews?'

'You don't have to do it if you don't want to,' I told him. 'There's no way he can make you do it.'

'Have another beer, kid,' said Eustace. 'It'll make you feel better! Percherons are no different from quarters – only bigger. It ain't difficult once you learn the trick to it. Aaah – you'll be good at it I tell you!'

Jacob was not listening to him. He was still watching me. 'Dr Matthews,' he said, 'tell me – am I crazy?'

I was in no mood to answer that question.

Jacob and I had another beer apiece, and Eustace had another rye, before we went outside to see the percheron. It was in the van I had seen when we went into the saloon. This truck was actually a stable on wheels: the rear doors opened downwards to form a runway, the inside walls were padded, there was a stall and a bale of fodder – it was something to see. And the percheron itself was a gorgeous animal. It stood at least nineteen hands high and it had the most beautiful white mane I've ever seen. I was impressed.

'You mean I have to ring Frances Raye's doorbell and then just give this thing to her?' Jacob gasped. He was really worried. 'What if she isn't home?'

Eustace was casually lighting a cigarette. 'Then you go back tomorrow night,' he said. 'I'll give you another twenty-five dollars. If she isn't home it won't be your fault.'

'What will I do with the horse then?'

'If you can't deliver it, the driver will take it back to the stables. Then you can tell him when you want it tomorrow night and he'll bring it around to your door.'

They locked up the back of the truck and Eustace went around to the front, and stood talking to the driver. Jacob had thrust his hands deep into his topcoat pockets and was looking glum.

'I'm not crazy, doc – am I? You see him, too – don't you? He's real – isn't he?'

'You don't have to go through with this absurd joke, you know,' I told him. 'You don't need the money. It's my opinion that one of your friends is trying to make a fool of you. I wouldn't let him get away with it if I were you.' I spoke quickly, angrily. Jacob's vacillating attitude was aggravating – particularly as I was not sure that the joke was not being played on me.

Jacob stood there, fingering the hibiscus in his hair. 'Oh, I'll have to do it tonight,' he said. 'Eustace is counting on me and I can't let him down! But I'm not so sure I'll do it after this . . . Percherons are a little too big . . .'

I was exasperated. He still might be a neurotic, and I still might be a physician bound by my Hippocratic oath – but the odds were that he was only a silly, impressionable youth that someone was playing a long, drawn-out, unfunny practical joke on. And there I was, standing on a street corner, trying to reason with him. I felt insulted!

'At least you can take that silly flower out of your

hair!' I said peevishly, knowing well that it was the last thing I should have said at that time but not being able to keep myself from saying it. 'You don't have to make yourself doubly ridiculous!'

That did it. If I still stood a chance of arguing him out of his foolish risk, I threw it away by taunting him. He was immediately on his dignity – I saw his shoulders stiffen – although he was too proud to let me know I had hurt him. Instead he let me have the full benefit of that off-centre grin. 'Oh, no, I couldn't do that,' he said. 'That wouldn't be fair to Joe. Besides I'm used to having a flower in my hair. I sort of like it.'

I gave up. There is never any point in arguing with a neurotic about his obsession – not that I was convinced Jacob was a neurotic. If he ever changes, the change will come from within himself. All the doctor can do is to point it out. Jacob was either a foolish youth who was too absurdly proud to admit he was an object of ridicule, or his neurosis was so ingrown that I could not instil a desire for change. Perhaps he preferred to be neurotic. It would not be the first time I had met the symptom. If later he thought differently, he knew where he could get in touch with me. As for now, he could go ahead and give Frances Raye a percheron if that gratified any hidden urge in his psyche. I'd be damned if I'd have anything more to do with it!

I said good-bye, turned up my coat collar against the drizzle and walked down Third Avenue towards 59th Street and the crosstown car. I felt very put upon and badly used. As I ate a lonely dinner in the Columbus Circle Child's, it occurred to me that the police might be interested in Eustace's crazy scheme. Annoying an actress by tethering a percheron to her doorstep might easily be a misdemeanour, if not something worse. I thought about telephoning my old friend, Lieutenant

Anderson of the Homicide Division, and reporting the whole silly routine to him. But I soon decided against that. If nothing came of it, and no one ever tried to give Frances Raye a horse, Anderson would never stop laughing at me. So, instead, I went down to Penn Station, walked to Sixth Avenue and caught the tubes to Jersey.

And as I sat in the half-light of the underground, my ears filled with the rushing roar of pent-up steel on steel, I kept turning the whole wild muddle over and over in my mind. Soon I found I had lost my carefully nurtured objectivity, and with it my scoffing attitude. I was as much a part of Jacob's mental crisis as I believed Nan to be. This is not supposed to be a healthy state of mind for a psychiatrist, but I am not too sure. How can one understand or appreciate the trauma of a neurotic if one has never experienced similar trauma oneself? I knew I would not sleep well that night – I was all but resigned to the fact that I would not sleep well any night until my patient showed definite improvement. And I was ashamed of myself for leaving him alone with his dilemma.

If I forgot for an instant the disturbing fact that at least Eustace, and that part of Jacob's story was real, it would be a simple matter to name his complaint. He was verging on schizophrenia, if he weren't already a schizoid. But Eustace was real (and I had to admit to myself that later experience might prove Joe and Harry to be equally real); he and his peculiar proclivity for paying Jacob to give away silver quarters and blooded horses were not an irrational fancy. At this point, I could not get past that improbable fact unless I doubted my own sanity.

And a psychiatrist must never doubt his own sanity.

*   *   *

I did fall asleep that night, but only after tossing for what seemed hours. I did not get to sleep for long though. Sara's voice, sleepy and irritable, awakened me.

'The telephone is ringing, George!' she said. 'Ringing its head off! Please go answer it!'

I groped for my slippers, threw my bathrobe over my shoulders and stumbled down the stairs. The voice over the wire was Nan's. If I had been sleepy before, as soon as I understood what it was she was saying I was instantly awake.

'Jacob's been arrested, doctor!' she said. 'In connection with the murder of Frances Raye! They found her dead in her apartment, and him, outside, drunk, ringing her doorbell, trying to get in! Oh, doctor, they think he killed her!'

All I could think to ask her was: 'What did he do with the horse?'

3

A QUESTION OF MOTIVATION

I reached Centre Street about six o'clock in the morning. Before I saw Jacob I had a talk with Lieutenant Anderson of the Homicide Division. Anderson was a man I liked; I had served as consultant on several cases with him and I respected his intelligence. He was a dour, middle-aged man with sparse grey hair. His face had a certain lean spareness that was the only trace of the officer of the law to be found in his manner or appearance; otherwise he resembled a dyspeptic businessman.

I was not prepared for the cold way he greeted me. He did not look up when I came into his office. He was bent over his desk writing; I stood for a minute or so waiting for him to ask me to sit down, and then I sat down anyway. I had used the same technique myself on occasion and I knew its uses and why it was sometimes necessary – it was one of the best ways to give yourself an initial advantage in an interview. Perhaps, this was why it angered me. I already felt rather put upon about the entire affair, but I had not expected Anderson – whom I considered a personal friend – to treat me this way. I decided I could keep silent as long as he could. I refused to allow myself to be restless or to look at him. Yet I knew he was watching me.

'They tell me Jacob Blunt is a patient of yours, George.' Anderson spoke when I least expected him to and, despite myself, I was startled.

'Since yesterday afternoon. I saw him for the first time yesterday,' I answered.

'What was the matter with him last night? Was he drunk or is he crazy?'

'I shall have to see him and examine him before I can say that,' I said.

'Cautious, aren't you?'

Anderson's way of speaking had always been terse, drily humorous on occasion, but never impolite. He was not being impolite now, for that matter. In his last curt question, I detected a hint of amused recognition of my own confusion. The difference in his manner, I decided, lay in the difference in our relationship – perhaps, even in the difference in my own point of view. Heretofore I had been a consultant working with him on equal terms, but now I was a witness. With this thought I allowed myself to relax, to drop my defences. 'It might help me if you told me what happened last night,' I reminded him.

The Lieutenant's sharp, blue eyes regarded me steadily, but I suspected that he was suppressing a smile. Why, the fellow liked having to interrogate me! 'Frances Raye was murdered last night,' he said. 'Her body was found on the living-room floor of her apartment on West Tenth Street. It was near the door, about six paces away. She had been stabbed in the back. We haven't found the knife.'

'What has my patient to do with it?'

'Blunt's queer actions led to our discovery of the body. He was standing outside the house ringing the doorbell.

A big horse with a fancy mane was tethered to the nearest lamp-post. A scout car was passing by, and the boys thought the set-up looked funny. So they parked and investigated. Blunt told them a "leprechaun" had paid him twenty-five dollars to deliver the horse to Raye. The boys thought he was drunk, but one of them went inside to see if he had bothered Miss Raye. He found her door unlocked and her body on the floor.'

'What did Jacob say about that?'

'He said he didn't know anything about it. He kept repeating the same outlandish story about a "leprechaun" named "Eustace" who had given him the horse and paid him to deliver it to Raye. I questioned him myself about an hour ago and he said the same thing. Finally, I told one of the boys to lock him up until he came to his senses.'

'What's he charged with?'

'Drunk and disorderly.'

I was relieved. From what Nan had told me over the telephone, I had thought that Jacob was under suspicion of murder.

'Of course, he could have killed her,' Anderson went on. 'Or he could have seen the murderer on his way out. But when I talked to him, I got the idea he was more than drunk—' He tapped his forehead significantly.

'As I said before, I know very little about him – nothing more than I gained in a short interview yesterday afternoon – but if his mind is affected I doubt if his type of aberration would lead to homicide. Not so soon, at least,' I said.

'You mean this "leprechaun" he was talking about?'

I nodded my head. 'Something like that. He might have been suffering from hallucinations.'

Anderson leaned his head on his hand. 'The trouble is I don't have any clues. The door to her place was ajar, the

35

building doesn't have a desk clerk or elevator operator – just one of those buzzer arrangements – and even the front door was unlocked. If your booby killed her, why did he go back outside and ring her doorbell?'

'Anyone could have done it, is that it? Were there signs of struggle? Was anything stolen?'

Anderson stood up and came round his desk. He was a short man in a neat, double-breasted suit. He fingered his tie nervously, unloosing the knot. There was a button missing on his coat sleeve. 'No, the place was in apple-pie order and nothing seemed to be missing. Raye was wearing one of those backless négligés – not the sort of thing she would wear if she were expecting company, unless it was a certain kind of company. They tell me she didn't have anything on underneath.'

'What about her friends?' I asked. 'Are you going to question them?'

He smiled for the second time. Again I had the feeling that he enjoyed the advantage of his position. The next time he consulted me, I knew how I was going to act. 'We're taking care of that,' he said, and his tone let me know that I had asked a foolish question.

'Then you don't think Jacob murdered her?'

He shook his head. 'No, I don't.' He did not sound too happy about it. 'Nobody, even a nut, who had just killed a woman would try to get by with a preposterous alibi like that.' He shook his head again as if he still could not believe that Jacob had told him what he had. 'And even nuts have reasons for doing what they do, particularly murder. Crazy reasons, but still reasons.'

'And Jacob has no motive . . .'

He nodded his head glumly. 'That's about the size of it.'

'Lieutenant,' I said, 'what would you say if I told you

that I had met and talked to this leprechaun Jacob was telling you about? Eustace, I mean?'

He did not even look up at me. 'I'd say you were crazy, too.'

'But it's true. I met him only last night.' Then I went on to tell him about Eustace and the percheron. 'I heard him promise Jacob twenty-five dollars to bring the horse to Frances Raye,' I concluded.

I think that Anderson felt like quitting his job then – just throwing up his hands and walking away, never to return. His shoulders slumped and his eyes grew tired. For the first time he looked like a man who had been awakened in the middle of the night to investigate a murder. His manner seemed to say: 'There are some things no man can endure!' Well, it served him right for the way he had been acting to me. Now the shoe was on the other foot and I hoped it pinched!

'George, I must remind you that there are penalties attached to obstructing the course of justice,' he said, wearily clutching at the remains of his dignity.

'What I said was the truth. In every detail. On my professional honour. I told you because I thought the information might lead to something in connection with the case.'

Then I told him the story of Jacob's visit to my office the previous day and the events that followed. I ended by saying, 'I'm in a position similar to yours. I cannot believe these things to be true, and yet I cannot escape the evidence of my own senses. I cannot say whether we are dealing with a wily madman or the ingenuous victim of a vicious conspiracy!'

Anderson slumped down in his chair. He seemed discouraged. I felt tired and over-tense myself. The lack of sleep suddenly began to weigh on me, the four dreary walls of the small office oppressed me. I wanted to get up and walk out – to forget all about it.

'We have to find this "Eustace,"' said Anderson. 'We have to make him talk – tell who hired him and all the details. Then we may get to the bottom of it.'

'Who do you think is behind it?' I asked.

He shook his head. 'I don't know. I haven't an idea.'

'We can't get at Eustace without Jacob's help,' I reminded him. And a moment later I regretted that I had spoken. The same thought entered both of our minds at once. Anderson looked at me, a smile creasing his saturnine face. Then he sat down and began to play with the pencils on his desk.

'If I release him into your custody, will you work with him and try to find out what he knows? I'll give you any police assistance you may need.'

This was what I had feared he would suggest. I did not want to do it. I wanted to be done with Jacob and his little men. And yet I was curious. 'What about my practice?' I asked. 'It would take time and I have a long list of appointments every day.'

'You'll get paid for your time. Any fee within reasonable limits.'

I wanted to do it, and I didn't want to. I felt a responsibility towards Jacob – if I did not do it he might be prosecuted for a crime he did not commit – and yet I had no desire to get entangled with Eustace and Joe and Harry. It was difficult for me to say either yes or no.

At last I made up my mind. 'I'll do it,' I said, 'if we can start now. I want to lose as little time from my practice as possible.'

Anderson pressed a button on his desk. He was smiling. 'You can find out what he knows if anyone can, George,' he said. 'I've always liked working with you.'

I said nothing, but I was amused by the change in his manner. Now that I had agreed to do what he wanted me to do, there was no need for him to dissimulate and we were friends again. 'I'll give orders to release Blunt into your custody. If you could get him to open up and talk to you by – say – this afternoon, that would be fine.'

I held up my hand. 'Not so fast,' I said. 'It's going to take longer than that.' I was thinking of how unsuccessful I had been the day before when I had tried to find out what was really wrong with Jacob.

'Well, report your progress and his whereabouts every day.'

'And, in the meantime, what will you be doing?' I asked him.

'I'll be working at it from this end. I'll let you know how that goes, too.'

I found Nan waiting for me in the corridor outside Anderson's office. She was a subtly different person from the girl I had met the night before; although she was every whit as beautiful, her manner was no longer as intense – she seemed withdrawn, distracted.

'What did he say?' she asked me, and, strangely enough, she averted her eyes. I had the feeling that she did not care to know.

'Anderson is releasing Jacob to me. They should be bringing him up in a few minutes. I'll be responsible for him – he will have to stay with me, but he will be out of jail.'

'How did you manage to work that?' Her exclamation was automatic, her voice apathetic. I looked at her curiously. She looked away again.

'I've known Anderson for several years,' I said. 'I worked with him as a psychiatric consultant on a number of cases. So I pointed out to him that parts of Jacob's story were clearly true, and to get the whole truth we would have to get Jacob to confide in us. Anderson realizes that psychiatric methods sometimes work in places where police methods fail. He's releasing Jacob – although he will still be technically under arrest – under my supervision. Jacob is not yet out of the woods, though.'

'I suppose it's like being out on bail?' Again she spoke lifelessly and gave me the impression that none of this mattered to her. I stared at her, remembering the impulsive, prying interest she had shown in my opinion of Jacob just the previous evening. She saw that I was puzzled and smiled at me. 'Don't mind my mood, doctor. I'll snap out of it. So many things have happened in so short a time that I guess it's all been a little too much for me.'

'You should go home and rest,' I said. 'I can see how this has affected you.'

'I'm all right now, or I shall be as soon as I have some breakfast. I don't want to go home now. I want to be with you when you meet Jacob.'

Oddly enough, she sounded as if she meant her last statement.

A few minutes later a man came down the corridor toward us, accompanied by a policeman. He was about thirty, of middle-size, with slick black hair and an annoyingly small moustache. As soon as Nan saw him, she rushed to meet him, throwing her arms about him and crying, 'Darling, they aren't holding you any longer. Dr Matthews is going to be responsible for you!'

But the man she was kissing, the man she had called 'darling', was not Jacob Blunt. He was not the man who had come into my office the previous afternoon and who had later introduced me to Eustace. His hair was not even the same colour.

There was something very wrong.

I waited to see what would happen. I knew I could do one of two things: either denounce him to Anderson on the spot, or let him think I did not know that a substitution had taken place and see if I could learn something important. I knew then and there that the sensible thing for me to do was to tell him that I did not know him, that he was not Jacob Blunt. But I hated to face Anderson again, to make myself doubly ridiculous. If I could find out what lay behind the muddle of Jacob, the little men and their preposterous activities, I might be able to turn the tables on Anderson. I was still brooding about being awakened in the middle of the night to rush down to Centre Street only to be questioned like a common criminal by my old friend. As a result, what I did may not seem intelligent – all I can say is that it made sense to me then, it even looked like a good idea. I walked down the corridor to a desk, signed some papers and then walked out of the station with Nan and 'Jacob'. He did not say anything until we were standing outside on the street.

'It was funny my finding her body like that,' he said, self-consciously. 'I don't blame the cops for thinking I did her in.'

'You didn't, of course?'

He looked at me, feigning incredulity. He was smiling, but his face was pale and his mouth worked nervously. 'You don't think I killed her, do you? My God, I didn't! I really didn't!'

'Why shouldn't I think so? You were the one person who was found near the scene of the crime.' I thought

41

I was testing him. I wanted to see how far his bravado would carry him before he realized that I knew he was an impostor.

We had been walking down the street. He stopped and took Nan's hand in his, pulling her around roughly so that she faced him. I saw the flesh of her wrist turn white under the pressure of his fingers, and I thought I saw her wince. 'You don't think that of me, darling – do you?' he demanded.

Nan would not look at him. 'I don't know, Jacob. I'm not sure.'

He turned to me. His eyes were cold, but his mouth was uneasy. I saw that he did not know how to take my acceptance of him as Jacob Blunt. Whatever he had expected, it was not this.

'But, doc, I didn't do it I tell you! I did get drunk last night with Eustace. I did serenade Frances Raye and try to break down her door. But I never killed her, honest I didn't! Why, I'd never seen her before last night!'

I could not understand what he hoped to gain by pretending he was Jacob. Although he succeeded in imitating Jacob's voice and way of talking fairly well, I was certain that this man was not the man who had visited my office. And by this time I had decided that as soon as I could get to a telephone, I would call Anderson and tell him what had happened.

We continued to walk up the street to the I.R.T. station. I kept on the look-out for a drugstore or lunch wagon that had a telephone, but all I saw were office buildings. Then it struck me that if I made a call now, it would be too obvious. I had better wait until we arrived at my office and I could excuse myself for a moment. During this time neither Nan nor Jacob spoke. This in itself was strange since Nan had struck me as being rather talkative. We walked down the steps of the subway entrance and stood on the platform waiting for the Uptown Local. From far off came the beginnings of a metallic roar – the train was approaching. I remember thinking: I can watch him on the train to see if he resembles my patient in any particular. I remember sensing that someone near me had moved, that someone else had whispered words that had something to do with me. I remember beginning to turn around, the first sensation of fright . . . and at the same instant I knew that the grinding roar had increased and that the two gleaming lights of the train were almost level with me . . .

Then I felt a sharp blow in the middle of my back. I remember arching, grabbing at air – I remember twisting, falling against something that rushed past me and tore me away with it and then threw me down . . .

4

NON COMPOS MENTIS

Two eyes were looking down at me. Two cold blue eyes
in a fat womanish face. No lipstick. No rouge. A pallid,
fleshy pancake of a face.

'Open your mouth.'

I opened my mouth and a cold thing went into it. I
peered down my nose to see what it was and my head
was one solid stabbing pain. The face swam away from
me accompanied by a harsh, rustling sound, leaving me
looking at a very flat pale green wall. Very flat indeed.

Was it a wall? Could it be a ceiling? But if it were
a ceiling, I must be lying on my back! What would I
be doing lying on my back looking at a very flat pale
green ceiling?

The face was back again. It was even closer than
before. The cold thing, now warm, slid mysteriously
backward out of my mouth. I did not like the face. I
wished it would go away.

After the face went away, I decided that the cold thing
must have been a thermometer . . . and that I must be
sick . . . in bed . . . in a hospital? I would ask the face.

* * *

45

I waited a long time for the nurse to return. And when she did, I found I could scarcely speak. The first time I tried I only made a rushing sound. My mouth was dry as felt and my tongue was twice its normal size, awkward, an impediment to speech. I tried to speak again. I managed to say, 'Nurse!'

'Yes.'

'Where am I?'

'You're sick. But never mind. You'll be all right.'

I closed my eyes. The effort had been too much. I had wanted to find out something . . . something important. But now it did not matter.

The next time I awoke I felt better. My head still ached, but it was easier to think and my mouth felt more natural. This time I waited eagerly for the nurse. I still could not remember what was so important, but I wanted to ask questions. I wanted to find out the name of the hospital. I wanted to know what had happened to me.

The nurse did not come.

After a while another face came. A blank, lined face such as I had seen many times before but could not remember where. Cold brown eyes like flawed marbles. A mouth that twitched.

'Aggie's got you too!' it said. 'Like me, Aggie's come and got you too. And you ain't goin' to get away! Naaah! You ain't goin' to get away. Aggie's got you!'

The face laughed. I felt sorry for it, but I did not know why. I had seen so many like it before, but where? The face kept on laughing.

'They come for me too,' it said. 'They come in a wagon. They drug me. Yaah, they drug me! Oh, I didn't wanta go, but they made me.' And then suddenly the face began to whimper – the mouth trembled and the brown marbles glistened with tears. 'Never done no harm. Never hurt nothin'. Why should they hurt me? Why should Aggie get me? Never done no harm . . .'

A flat toneless voice that went on and on. I shut my eyes. Would the nurse never come?

The third time I awakened I knew where I was. I must have felt stronger because I tried to sit up. I could not. I could only move my head. I was strapped to my bed. That could only mean one thing: I was in the psychopathic ward of a hospital.

That explained the second face. A paranoiac. I had seen many just like that in my days at the sanatorium – I had even encountered a few in private practice. They were unmistakable: the empty, neurotic face, the unending complaint of the toneless voice, the humourless, mechanical laugh . . .

But what was I doing in a mental ward? I was not insane. I was a psychiatrist. Who had committed me?

The fat face again. This time it was easier to talk.

'Where am I?'

'You're sick. Don't talk.'

'But what's the name of the hospital? Where am I?'

'Be quiet. Be a good boy . . .'

The last word held as if the sentence might not be finished.

'But where am I? What am I doing here?'

The fat face was gone.

This time I was determined to find out where I was and why. They could not keep me, a doctor – a psychiatrist – in ignorance like this. It was unethical. I would demand to see the doctor in residence.

After a long wait another face appeared. A competent

face with glasses, a professional face, a man's face – the doctor?

'Where am I?'

'The City Hospital.'

'The psychopathic ward?'

'Yes.'

'But, doctor, you can't keep me here!'

'I'm afraid we have to, old man.'

'My name's Matthews, George Matthews. I'm a doctor with offices on Lexington Avenue. I'm a psychiatrist.'

He hesitated before he spoke. 'Your name is John Brown. Homeless. Picked up wandering.'

'It's not true! It's as I told you! I'm a physician, a psychiatrist. You can't treat me like this!'

'I'm afraid you're mistaken, old boy. But I'll look into it. "George Matthews," did you say?'

'Doctor, I tell you—'

But he was gone.

He came back.

'Who did you say you were?'

'Dr George Matthews of 445 Lexington Avenue and Hackensack, New Jersey.'

'There is such a doctor. How did you know his name? Has he treated you at some time?'

It did not look like a stupid face – how could it be so obtuse? I wanted to shout at it, but I knew I must keep calm, a model of sanity.

'I am that man, doctor. Look, you can call a number, can't you? You can call Butterfield 2-6888, can't you? That won't do any harm.'

'But that's Dr Matthews' number.'

'That's what I'm telling you! I am Dr Matthews! There's been a mistake. Call that number and describe me to my nurse. If the description tallies, you will know I'm telling the truth!'

The face was gone. To telephone I hoped.

This time he was back quickly. The first I knew of his presence was when I felt the straps loosen. I sat up. A young, embarrassed intern stood at the foot of my bed. He was not smiling.

'Well,' I said, 'I was right, wasn't I?'

Only then did it occur to me that I might not be right. An irrational fear, I told myself. I knew who I was, didn't I?

'I was mistaken—' he began.

'That's what I was trying to tell you . . .'

He spoke quickly. 'I was mistaken in saying there is a Dr George Matthews,' he said. 'There was a Dr George Matthews. But he died recently.'

He spoke clearly and distinctly. Underlining each simple sentence as if he were speaking to a child. Or a madman.

'What do you mean?'

'I looked first in an old directory. Then I found a Dr George Matthews at the address you gave me. But when I called the number, exchange cut in and said there was no such number. I checked with a later directory and I found that Dr George Matthews had died.'

'When?'

'I don't know when. Between this year and last, I suppose.'

'But I am Dr George Matthews. I'm not dead. I live in Hackensack, New Jersey. I have a wife named Sara . . .'

The intern was very embarrassed. He gripped the foot of my bed with both his hands, clenched the rail tightly as if he were fighting pain. 'I'm afraid you're mistaken. I know it seems that way to you, but that is not your name. Our records are quite accurate – I checked them again before I came back. The name on your Social Security Card, which we found in your pocket, is that of John Brown.'

Then he went away. What was the use of telling him I had never had a Social Security Card? He knew that they had never been issued to doctors just as well as I did.

They let me up and around but would not let me shave myself. They gave me an old pair of corduroy trousers, the ones I had been wearing – I was told – when they found me. I held them up with my hands. I could not have a belt because I might hang myself with it. There was no mirror, and I was not allowed to leave the ward. I could not see what I looked like now.

By running my hand over my head I could tell that my hair was more closely cropped than it used to be. It felt short and bristly like an undergraduate's. I began to feel like a different man, a poor man, a sick man.

I grew friendly with the young intern. His name was Harvey Peters. We talked together whenever he could spare the time. I argued with him again and again. But it never did any good.

On the second day –

'Doctor, I tell you my name is Matthews! I am married and I live in Hackensack, New Jersey. I want you to get in touch with my wife.'

'I'll try if you want me to.'

'There must have been some mistake about the other. The telephone company's error. But reach my wife, please! She'll be worrying about me.'

'I'll try—'

The third day –

'My wife's coming to see me today? You got in

touch with her, didn't you? She'll be coming to take me home today?

He shook his head. 'I'm sorry, fellow. I tried. But I could not reach your wife.'

'She wasn't in? She was out shopping most likely. Sara likes to shop. But you'll try again? She'll be in the next time you call.'

'There is no Mrs George Matthews in the Hackensack telephone book.'

'But, doctor, we have a phone. I know we have a phone.'

He kept shaking his head. I could see he pitied me now. 'There is no Mrs George Matthews in Hackensack, New Jersey, who is a doctor's wife. That Mrs George Matthews moved away. She left no forwarding address. I know because I've checked with the post office.'

'Doctor, there must be some mistake! She wouldn't leave like that – without a word!'

'I'm sorry, old man. You're mistaken.'

'I'm not mistaken. I am George Matthews.'

'You must not get so excited. You must rest.'

Another day –

'Doctor, how long have I been here?'

'About two weeks.'

'What is the diagnosis?'

'Amnesia, with possible paranoid tendencies.'

'But I know who I am! It's just that I can't prove it!'

'I know. I know that's the way it seems.' He was humouring me. A mild-mannered, kind, young man who was almost a doctor was humouring me. He pitied me. He had not as yet developed the necessary callousness and the aberrations of his more intelligent patients still dismayed him. He wanted to let me down gently. I knew he would comply with all my requests (or pretend to comply), because he felt that my interest in my former life – in any former life, even a mythical one – was an encouraging symptom, a sign of possible improvement.

I continued to batter my hopes against this blind construction of theory and tradition, this man for whom I was mad because my history sheet said I was – and if I were not psychotic, why then was I in the psychopathic ward of the hospital?

'But, doctor,' I said, 'I know who I am. A man suffering from amnesia does not know who he is. All, or a part, of his past life is lost – he has misplaced his identity, his personal history, even his habits. That isn't a description of me!'

He answered me patiently. He talked while his eyes looked past me, remembering the definitions and practices learned by rote, mechanically interposing the logical objections, the proper refutation to all my proposals. A neurotic catechism – a litany for the irrational!

'You do not recognize your identity. You do not recognize your name – worse! – you refuse to accept it as yours. You put forward instead another man's name, a dead man's name, and claim it as your own. You claim his wife, his profession. And, building on this delusion, you begin to think that all of us are persecuting you, holding back what is rightfully yours. That is paranoia.'

'Doctor, do me a favour?'

'What is it?'

'Call the police. Headquarters. Ask to speak to Lieutenant Anderson of the Homicide Division. Tell him I am here. Describe me to him. Tell him that there has been a mistake – that something has gone badly wrong.'

'But the police brought you here. You were charged with vagrancy. The police know all about you.'

'Just this one last favour, doctor. Please, call Lieutenant Anderson!'

He went away. This time I did not pretend to myself. This time I knew that it would do no good. Although I might still have him call my club and some of the medical societies I belonged to, I suspected that the response would always be the same. This was the last time I would try. After this I could do nothing but wait.

He returned, stood at the foot of my bed, hesitant, sorry for me. 'Lieutenant Anderson knew Doctor Matthews well,' he said. 'He committed suicide last year. His body was found in the North River. The Lieutenant said that you must be an impostor.'

After that I began to believe it myself.

It was terrifyingly easy for me to believe that the past that I remembered was unreal. I had been lifted out of my life as totally as a goldfish is dipped out of an aquarium; more so, for when a storekeeper scoops a fish he soon places it again in a paper bucket of water – the fish remains in its element. I was not so fortunate. I lived and breathed, but in an entirely different fashion, horribly unfamiliar.

They wake you early in a mental hospital, at about six o'clock. They feed you prunes, oatmeal, wholewheat bread, butter, coffee. Then you help clean up the ward until nine o'clock. You make your bed, you push a mop, you scrub toilets. There is enough for an hour's work, but you have until nine o'clock to do it. But that is not too long. After a while, it takes you until nine o'clock because from nine until twelve is the rest period. That means you have nothing to do between nine and twelve but rest. You sit. You listen to the radio. Sermons, recipes, the news every hour on the hour. If there is an old magazine or newspaper around, you read it even if you have read it from cover to cover ten times before. What is left of it, that is. All items that might have an exciting or depressing effect on the patients have been removed.

The big room is clean. It is warm. There are comfortable wicker chairs (made by the patients – occupational therapy), and outside the sun is shining.

This is all necessary. I knew it to be necessary, knew for a fact that I was in a model institution, but knowing it did not help me to accept. After a week, two weeks, more weeks of sitting and listening, you get so you listen, wait to hear a sound different from the rest. The sense of hearing is the last to give up hope. But you know that time will never end, and you begin to scheme against this fact, to plan lovely lies of escape and the return to a life that probably never existed. For after twelve comes lunch, a stew of meat and potatoes, wholewheat bread, butter, jello. And after lunch you clean the toilets again, push the mop (if you have mechanical aptitude you can go to the shop) until three – and after three there is a rest period until five. Then you have supper, a piece of beef or a bowl of soup, wholewheat bread, butter, rice pudding. And after supper you go to bed and tell lies to yourself until you go to sleep.

On Thursdays I saw the psychiatrist – a pleasant woman, Dr Littlefield, a behaviourist. She gave me tests. Fit the little pegs into the little holes, the big pegs into the big holes. Turn the discs over and put them back in place – one side red, one side white – see how quickly you can do it! Answer the questions, as many as you can. A king is a monarch, serf, slave, hedonist, a lucky man. Underline the one you think is more nearly right: $2 \times 2 + 48 = 54, 62, 57, 52$.

She was a small woman with a bun of neat brown hair. Her eyes were blue and she had a tidy smile. I guessed she was about my age. The first time I did the tests, she studied my paper carefully, biting her lip as she evaluated it. I waited eagerly to hear her say: Why there must be some mistake! Why nobody in a mental hospital should do this well!

I should have known better. She looked up at me and smiled politely. 'You show ready understanding. I think you have no trouble learning. But there is a certain instability indicated – a compulsion?'

A sane man could have taken the same tests and made the same answers. A sane man? I was a sane man. But did I think so? Could I really be deluding myself?

I wanted to tell her what I knew, prove to her that I, too, could give Stamford-Binet tests, make a prognosis, indicate treatment. I wanted to be a bright student. I wanted to outwit teacher. But I knew I did not dare.

There was only one way I could get out. I must show 'improvement'. It did not matter what the truth was. I could never prove to them that my name was George Matthews, that I was a doctor, a psychiatrist, a married man with a bank account. Or if I could it would take a very long time. I knew that what I would have to do would be to break down all the individual, carefully constructed ramparts of science and knowledge – I would have to prove to Dr Littlefield, Dr Peters, Nurse Aggie Murphy, that I was a man and not a case history, a human and not a syndrome. And I could not allow myself a short time. I had to get out tomorrow, or the day after, or the day after that!

I realized this when Peters reported my own suicide to me. He told me that Anderson had said I died last year – *last year*. I took that piece of information, so casually dropped, and with equal calm stored it in a cranny of my mind. I must have lost months! When I looked outside I saw that it was summertime. I must actually have had a loss of memory (that rushing blackness in the subway seemed yesterday or last week, not last year – but I knew it had happened on a rainy fall day, the 12th October). The problem was: had I forgotten the same period they thought I had? Amnesia cuts two ways. You can forget your remote past, your early years, childhood, youth, young manhood, or you can forget a piece of your maturity.

I knew now that I had forgotten some things – I did not realize how much.

But I could lie. I could build a past that was not true, but which fitted the role I had been given. I could report the fictional history of a destitute man, and I could do it well because I had studied and put to heart many such case histories.

They expected me gradually to recover my memory. Harvey Peters said that I showed improvement. Dr Littlefield gave me tests each Thursday and told me that I showed less fear, less anxiety. But they would never, or only after too long a time, know me for the man I was. Or had been.

Why should I be Dr George Matthews any longer? What was wrong with being John Brown? Someone wanted me to be John Brown. Why should I fight him?

Was identity worth slow decay?

No. I would lie.

I had made up my mind.

A year contains 365 days. I died last year. Dr George Matthews died this minute. John Brown is born. John Brown will escape. John Brown will find the one who wanted to obliterate Dr George Matthews – and who played with him first, twitting him with comedy! – and John Brown will destroy him.

'I was born in Erie, Pennsylvania. My father worked in the mills. I had seven brothers. My mother died. My sister ran away. I joined the Army under another name.'

'You remember now?'

'It comes back slowly. I was hurt – somewhere in France. I came home. There were no jobs. I was on relief. I went from town to town. I worked on farms up and down both coasts. Then I was away for a while.'

'Away? Just away?'

Slick, glib lies. I had to hide something. I had to make my story fit the pattern she expected, and she expected me to try to hold back some part of the whole.

'I got married. Down South. I worked for a real estate office. Then times got hard again. She was having a child. She should have had an operation. We waited too long. We didn't have the money for the operation. She died.'

'I'm sorry.'

A facile lie told slowly – a typical syndrome of self-pity. This was what was expected. This was what she was going to get.

For a few moments I said nothing. Dr Littlefield was respectfully silent. I wanted to laugh deeply. Life was bitter and good and I hated all of them. I was glad I knew how to lie.

'Then what happened?' Tentatively. Ready to take it back with silence if her timing was off. She did not want to precipitate an emotional block. This bland little trained priestess of scientific black magic thought she could steal my story from my unwilling mind. And it was I who was doing the embezzling!

'I left town. I went the rounds again. Things got worse. You know how it was during the Depression? In season I became a harvest hand. In the winter I stayed in cities – the relief is better there. I worked on the PWA, the WPA. I bummed around . . .'

Looking down, as if I were ashamed. I was not ashamed. Even if this had been my life, I would not have been ashamed.

'Yes?'

'I drank.'

'Much?'

'A lot.'

She did not say anything. Had I overplayed my hand?

'It's funny but I never want a drink any more.'

That ought to do it!

'No?'

'No, not since the bust on the head . . .'

I hoped the location was right. It was usually the head.

'When did you hurt your head?' She thought she was helping me remember! It was working!

'Before I came here. I had a fight. Over a woman. He came at me with a bottle. That's all I remember.'

A classic tale. Cribbed from a million sordid lives. But it would do.

Of course, they did not let me go right away. I had to run the gauntlet every day for a week. Dr Littlefield saw me again, then Dr Smithers and Dr Goldman. Harvey asked me sly questions. I fed them all the same pap. A detail here, a detail there. Careful parallels drawn from selected casework. Never too close, but always the pattern they had been taught to expect.

It worked. One day Dr Littlefield told me, 'You are much better. We think you are almost well. How would you like to leave us this week?'

A carefully nurtured smile. Must not be too much of a shock, but at the same time patient should be made to feel the doctor is pleased with his recovery.

'That would be nice. You really mean it?' Equally carefully contrived incredulity. Doctor must be made to feel patient's relief and pleased amazement, but doctor must not be allowed to perceive that the game has become very, very boring.

'Friday. You're to see Miss Willows today. I think she has a surprise for you.'

I was not surprised to find Miss Willows fat and sloppy. Social workers so frequently are. This was the woman who was to rehabilitate me! Well, I was willing.

'I've talked with Dr Littlefield about you,' she said. 'She tells me that you are thinking of leaving us?'

'Yes, ma'am.' I knew enough to be humble with her. Case-workers like humble people.

'We don't want you to go out and lead the life you've led before. Not that it's your fault. But if you will help yourself, we can help you.'

'Yes, ma'am.'

'A job in a cafeteria – not a very big job – but one with a good chance for advancement.'

'You're very kind, ma'am.'

'And if you work hard, and be sure to remember to report back to us every month the way Dr Littlefield told you – why there's no telling where you might end up!'

'Yes, ma'am. You're very kind, ma'am.'

On Friday, 12 July 1944, John Brown stepped on to a crosstown bus. In his pocket was the address of a Coney Island cafeteria where Miss Willows had told him to apply for a job as waiter and busboy. His clothes were cheap and new. His face was studiously blank. If you had looked at him closely, you would have said that he had once seen better days.

5

IN WHICH A MAN RUNS DOWN

From then on my name was John Brown. I could not explain, even to myself, the process by which I came to refute my identity. Not so long ago I had been a specialist with a comfortable living, a wife and a certain amount of status in the community. Now the world knew me only as a counterman in an all-night Coney Island cafeteria.

I had not intended to take the job Miss Willows offered me when I left the hospital that warm July day; there had been still some fight left in me. For weeks I had been shamming, assuming a false character, because I knew this to be the quickest way to return to what most of humanity considers sanity. I had been bitter during those weeks, cynical enough to adopt a fictional character and to play a hypocritical charade; but I had not lost hope. I might well have despaired if once in that time I had been allowed to look in a mirror.

I had noticed the lack of mirrors in the ward, but I had decided that this was a precaution similar to the banning of belts and braces: a mirror can be broken into sharp shards which can be employed to slit throats. Added care must have been taken to prevent my self-inspection in the last days of my convalescence; however, if it was, I was unaware. I do not blame Dr Littlefield for not letting me have a mirror, although if I had been in her place, I might have considered a confrontation a necessary part of my patient's adjustment. But, perhaps, this judgement is unfair: Dr Littlefield probably did not realize that I had not always been that way . . .

As it was I first caught sight of myself while having a coke in a drugstore, just after I descended from the bus that had taken me crosstown. Behind this soda fountain was a mirror, fancily decorated with gaudy signs urging the purchase of egg malted-milks and black-and-white sodas. I glanced up and looked into it without knowing what I was doing. My mind read the signs first, felt good at seeing a familiar sight while being as usual a little critical of the advertising profession. Then, when the signs were read, my consciousness became curious about the horribly disfigured man who must be sitting next to me. He was not old – about my age now that I studied his face – although he had seemed older at first glance. This was because his short-cropped hair was grey streaked with white and his jaw, that showed the remains of strength, trembled spasmodically. But what made him really fascinatingly ugly was the wide, long, angry red scar that traversed his face diagonally from one ear across the nose and down to the root of the jaw at the base of his other cheek. It was an old scar that had knit badly and in healing had pulled and twisted at the skin until the face it rode had the texture of coarse parchment and the grimace of a clown. One cheek, and the eye with it, was drawn sidewise and upward into a knowing leer – the other drooped, and with it a corner of the mouth, as if its owner were stricken with grief. The skin's colour was that of cigar ash, but the scar's colour was bright carmine. I pitied the man, then was embarrassed to look around at him; surely, he must have seen me staring at his reflection! But as I had this thought I noticed that his glass emptied itself of coca-cola just as I sucked noisily at my straw, and a suspicion crept into my mind. I fought it back, silently scoffed at it, and kept my eyes averted while I waited for my neighbour to go. How long I might have continued this self-deception I shall never know since I was soon forced to admit that the horribly mutilated face I had been staring at was my own. A little boy came in and sat down on the empty stool next to mine – it had been occupied only in my imagination – giggled, and said to his perspiring mother, 'Oh, mama, look quick at the man! Mama, how did he get like that?'

I fled with the child's taunt ringing in my ears. How did I get to be like this? I asked myself. And then, before I tried to answer that: How can I return to Sara like this?

I stopped in my tracks, stood staring out into the traffic. It would be so easy to run out into the street, to feel the crushing weight of a bus or truck, a blinding instant of pain, and then oblivion! My legs twitched with this necessity, a great hand pushed relentlessly at my straining back – I took two halting steps to the kerb, hesitated at its edge as if it were a precipice. My mouth went slack and the trembling of my jaw increased. Sweat trickled down my side from under my armpits.

Then, slowly, I turned and walked down the street towards a subway kiosk. John Brown, waiter or counter-man or busboy in a Coney Island eatery, belonged to that face. For the time being, I was John Brown. Dr George Matthews would remain in hiding at least a while longer. I did not know who had persuaded my wife that I had died, but she must have had good reason to think I had or else she would never have left the city.

Perhaps, it was better that way. Sara had a small income of her own, enough to take care of her. In the meantime I would have a chance to think things over. I laughed. Once I had been a psychologist and had thought myself capable of adjusting to any predicament. I fingered my scar, its treacherous smoothness – well, I was capable of an adjustment. In fact, I had already adjusted so completely that I was incapable of remembering the face that had preceded that tortured grimace seen in a fly-specked mirror. I had forsworn any personality other than 'John Brown, homeless, picked up wandering.'

I took the B.M.T. to Coney Island.

Mr Fuller was a small seedy-looking man with a scrubbed-pink face and bleary blue eyes. He looked like he might take one drink too many too often. The shirt he had on had probably been worn more than once, his tie was of sleazy imitation silk. His shoulders drooped, he looked harried. I know he did not mean to be unkind to me.

We sat down at one of the tables in the front of the cafeteria. It was the middle of the afternoon and the place was nearly empty. Outside the calliope of a merry-go-round wheezed and clanged and banged. A barker farther down the street exhorted a straggling, sweaty crowd of passers-by to 'Step right up and pay a dime to see "Zozo", the beautiful, delovely Latin who lives with a boa constrictor.' Mr Fuller paid no attention to these sounds. He fingered my slip of paper, studying it as if it were a text. He regarded it for such a long time that I began to debate the possibility that he would ever look up again; where-upon he coughed once, squirmed, blew his nose.

'Ever work in a cafeteria before, Mr—' (here he glanced at the slip of paper) '—Brown?'

'No, sir.' I had better say 'sir'. Now that I had decided

to remain John Brown, I would have very little money. Dr George Matthews' resources were no longer open to me – if they ever had been – and getting this job was all important.

'How do I know you can do the work? I'm not used to inexperienced help,' he complained.

'I'm good with people. I know how to talk to them. I have patience.' As soon as I had said these words, I was sure they were the wrong ones and my heart sank.

'There's more to the job than that,' he said. He looked at me inquiringly. 'You gotta be careful, you know? I been having too much breakage lately. They don't like too much breakage.'

'"They"?' I asked.

'The company,' he explained. 'They come in a couple of times a week and look around. Once a month they take inventory. If there's been too much breakage I hear about it. I'd like to put you on, but I can't be too careful . . .'

I spoke slowly and distinctly, trying desperately to sound sincere. 'I'd be very careful,' I said. 'I wouldn't break anything.'

He looked at me for a long time, queerly. At first I did not understand what he was looking at. Then came the shock of recognition – my hand clutched at my face.

'People hardly notice it,' I said quickly, as the tortured image rose in front of my eyes and partially obscured his face. 'I don't think your customers would mind. They haven't on other jobs,' I lied.

He thought for a moment. I could see that the effort needed to make a decision was great for him. 'I admit it's hard to get a good, steady man these days. Maybe a fellow like you has a hard time getting jobs? Maybe, if you got a good job like this, you'd be steady?'

'I'll be steady.'

He thought again. He squirmed around in his chair. He blew his nose.

'Well, I'll try you for a week. If you work hard and apply yourself, you may have a steady job. That is, if the customers don't complain.'

He stood up and walked to the rear of the cafeteria. I followed him. He gave me two clean aprons, a pair of white duck trousers and a black leather bow-tie. Then he told me to report for work at six o'clock that night. My hours would be from six until two, when I would be relieved. We shook hands and I thanked him. Then I left the place to go look for a room.

During the next month, the sultry, crowded days of August, I worked at the cafeteria six nights a week, slept or sat on the beach and read in the daytime, existed. I would be lying to say that this was an unhappy period. Indeed, I might say the opposite. I had no desire to do anything else. The books I read were adventure stories and the like. I did not dream of my former life, or of an impossibly satisfying one to come. I made no friends or enemies. Yet – if a form of contentment that was not unlike a drug-induced stupor can be called happiness – I was happy.

I had promised myself a period of time 'to think things over'. Yet I thought nothing over, made no decisions. Some day I might try again to be Dr George Matthews, the eminent young psychiatrist. Some day I would return to Sara – Sara, my heart quickened at the thought of her. Yet day after day went by, and I did nothing.

Several times in the first weeks I worked at the All-Brite I experienced recurring fits of self-consciousness. I would suddenly become acutely aware of my disfigurement (perhaps, a customer would stare at me too long), and I would leave my work, go to the lavatory and peer at my face in the looking-glass. In time, though, the first horror of my discovery passed and there came in its place a peculiar, perverted sense of pride in my distinction. No other quality of my adopted personality differed in the least from that of any man I might meet on the street or find sitting on the beach. In all other ways I was cut out of the same bolt of cloth as everyone else: I had a small job, I was lonely, I had little security. But I did have a bright scar on my face, and this disfigurement soon stood in my mind as a symbol of my new identity. I was John Brown, and as John Brown I had a scar that ran from my ear across my face diagonally. It was a strangely satisfying attribute.

There were times when a little of my old objectivity returned to me and I stood aside and looked at myself in self-appraisal; but these times were rare and soon they stopped altogether. I knew that being proud of a defect was a defence, a stepping-stone to neurosis, but I did not care. I concentrated on my tasks, saw to it that there was always one piece of each variety of pie on the counter, sufficient shaved ice on the salad trays and that the water was changed every hour in the percolators. I waited on trade and learned to be obsequious to get nickel and dime tips. And in all this time the thought of Sara, the home that had been ours, my practice and former prestige, was only a faint and annoying memory that came in the night like the ache of a hollow tooth and which I dismissed easily from my mind, ignored as I would any petty distraction. My life had become the product of my own distorted imaginings, and I did not dare let visions of a former reality disturb my precarious equilibrium, even though in my secret mind I may have longed for my former life.

Nor did I allow myself to think of Jacob Blunt. The whole warped history of Dr George Matthews' last day remained a forgotten thing. There are some memories we have, and which we are aware of, but never allow to become entirely conscious. Such memories are always lurking directly beneath the surface of our reason, and in times of crisis certain of our actions can only be explained in terms of these remembered experiences; yet they never become tangible and we never allow ourselves to speak of them in telling of our past. So it was with me regarding the details of Jacob Blunt and his 'little men' and the other vicious nonsense of that last day which may or may not have resulted in the death of Frances Raye and my accident in the subway. I knew they had happened but I chose to forget them. They were no part of my present life.

I even became proficient at my craft, if you can call being a counterman in a cafeteria a craft. There were three of us to a shift and each of us had a particular section of the counter to care for. The coffee urn, the salad table and the desserts were my province; it was my responsibility to see that the kitchen kept a sufficient quantity of these items on hand for me to replace the empty dishes as soon as the customers deplenished the stock. A simple job, but one that had its difficulties. Some of my troubles lay with the customers: patrons would insist on handling each of the sweets before choosing one or would demand special orders that took extra time to prepare and then get testy because they had to wait. Often it was the cook who was slow in preparing foods that were the most popular, while flooding me with huge quantities of the slower-moving delicacies. I worked out systems by which I could balance supply and demand, push butterscotch pie and sell less apple, get rid of the avocado salad when the avocados were not all they should be – systems that worked so well that the day came when Mr Fuller had a little talk with me and gave me a rise.

He stood behind me, watching me work and making me nervous. I heard him snuffle and blow his nose. He even cleared his throat before he said, 'They're pleased with the way you've turned out, Brown. Mighty pleased. Along with me they felt that maybe the customers would complain, but we haven't had any complaints. The breakage is down this month, too. You've turned out pretty well.'

'I try my best,' I said.

'They told me to tell you that they wanted you to stay with us, and not to get any foolish notions in your head about working some place else. We're going to raise your salary two dollars a week.'

He snuffled again and wiped his nose on an unclean handkerchief. Why should Fuller or his ever-present 'they' fear my leaving? Why should I look for another job? I was satisfied where I was.

The two dollars more a week meant nothing to me. I had been living on what I earned, spending it all on food, shelter, an occasional clean shirt, but needing nothing more. Now that I had it, I did not know what to do with it. Eventually, I put the extra money in my top bureau drawer, adding to it each week; not saving the way a cautious man saves with a goal in mind or for a prudent principle, but only putting it away because I had no desire to spend it and the bureau drawer seemed a more appropriate place than the wastebasket.

During the day and early evening the cafeteria was patronized by ordinary people out for a good time: small businessmen with their families, clerks with their girls, bands of teenage youngsters who dropped in for a hamburger and a coke and stayed long enough to be a nuisance. But after ten o'clock the character of the clientele changed radically. It was at this hour that the carnival people began to appear.

They were of all sorts and all kinds. Gaunt, under-nourished men would sidle up to the counter, order coffee and rolls, take their orders to a table and sit there the rest of the night. These were the less prosperous ones, the 'drifters'. They earned their livings by taking tickets, operating rides, selling hot-dogs and floss candy, by doing odd jobs. They sat with each other and did not mingle with the second group, the 'artists'.

Brassy blondes, flashily made-up red-heads, rarely a glossy-headed brunette, showgirls, wives of entrepreneurs, lady shills – all of these were considered 'artists'; as well as their masculine counterpart in checked suits and pointed-toe shoes, barkers, grifters who operated the 'sucker' games, pitch men and the 'big boys' who owned the concessions. The 'artists' came in later than the 'drifters', spent more money and were more convivial. They were a society to themselves, but a friendly, open-handed one; I learned that the 'drifters' did not mingle with them of their own choosing, not because the 'artists' were snobbish.

There was also a third group that kept partly separate, but also sometimes mixed with the shills and showgirls. Zozo, 'the delovely Latin who lives with a boa constrictor,' was a member of this clique, as was a man named Barney Gorham who kept a shooting gallery. Barney interested me very much. He was a great ape of a man with smoothed-back, glistening black hair and a half-grown beard. As he walked his shoulders would sway involuntarily; watching him one was always conscious of the movement of muscles beneath his rough flannel shirt. He would give the impression of having money when first met; and yet if one talked to him for any length of time he would invariably try to borrow a dollar or two. He pretended to be a painter, and it was true that he did paint in his spare time. Several times, when he brought them to the All-Brite, I saw some of his daubs; badly designed seascapes, highly romanticized pastoral scenes and gaudy portraits of those of the showgirls he had slept with. For Barney was successful with the 'ponies', as the ehorines were called. Usually, he had one or two girls with him, talking vivaciously, while he sat slumped in his chair glowering at the room.

I called these last the 'characters' and there were many of them, yet, of the three groups they were the most difficult to define and limit. A few of them were intellectuals or pseudo-intellectuals, and what they were doing at Coney Island I could not understand. Others were freaks; dwarfs and bearded ladies, the pin-headed boy who was really a cretin yet was accepted as a member of this loosely knit society – he was always accompanied by a large, motherly-looking woman with a monstrous goitre – a man who owned a motion picture theatre and a girl who ran a photographer's studio. I decided at last that what they all had in common was a sense of dissatisfaction. Both the 'drifters' and the 'artists' were content with their life, but the 'characters' – although many of them were successful financially – were malcontents. They were not peculiar to Coney Island except in their concentration; you might find small groups such as these in the theatrical district of any middle-western city. However widely they might be separated during the winter months, as each sought a way of earning a living (some by touring the South with a carnival, some by doing odd parts on Broadway or at Radio City, others by touting the race-tracks or taking any 'rube' job they could find), they always returned to this place in the summer, met at this cafeteria, considered this the centre of their lives.

I supposed it was only natural that after a time I came to be a part of this last group. John Brown was homeless too, and like everyone else needed to feel that he belonged. It cost nothing to sit down at one of the tables that had been designed to seat four, but around which six or seven were sitting, and soon I found myself joining in the conversations. These, instead of being confined to carnival gossip as I had guessed they might be, were about almost anything. I was surprised at how learned Barney was, for example, and both amused and frightened at the thought that Zozo, who lived with a boa constrictor, had not only read Kant but also Fichte and Spinoza. One of the favourite topics of discussion was psychoanalysis (it usually came up when one of the group would remember the time when the Wild Man from Borneo with Sells-Floto – 'a quiet type who liked Guy Lombardo and Wisconsin lager' – went berserk on the midway and killed three men – 'the show did great business for the rest of the stand, we made all the dailies and that year we went way over our nut'), and I astonished them with my knowledge of the field. While I restrained my memory of my past life, I seemed to have no compunction about using information I had gained during that life – in fact, one of the reasons why I was soon so fascinatedly a member of this odd group was because I was pleased to find so many neurotic personalities at one time. The All-Brite was a veritable game preserve for the psychiatric sportsman. Yet by the time I had worked in the cafeteria a month, I knew several of the 'characters' well enough to consider them my friends, and also to forget that I had once considered them eccentric.

Sonia Astart was one of my friends. She entered the

cafeteria at the same time each night, a few minutes after twelve. She would walk between the tables, speaking to this person or that, finally making her way to the counter where her order was always the same: a pot of black coffee. Then she would go sit with Barney or Zozo.

I joined Barney's table more often than I did the others, and Sonia was the reason for this. She seldom had much to say, but one never noticed her silence. When I was near her, I felt her presence and it was far more stimulating than words. Yet she had few of the standard hallmarks of womanly beauty. She was tall, and her features were irregular – she was not even especially fastidious. Often she was without lipstick or powder, sometimes the sloppy shirts and slacks she wore were badly in need of a pressing.

I am certain that there were times when Sonia did not know how she would manage to scrape enough money together to live the week. She was usually between jobs. And it was at these times that she would change from a listener to the most talkative of all those present. She had a marvellous fund of stories about the carnival folk, and she would talk politics or sex or a theory of art for hours on end with Zozo or myself or anyone who would argue with her, interrupting the discussion frequently to get up from the table, corner a prosperous-seeming friend who had just come in the door, speak long and earnestly with him for a few minutes, borrow money from him. It was as if she could not carry off the necessary wheedling, the tale of sudden, unexpected misfortune but certain better luck to come, without first plunging into the fever of argument. And when I considered the content of these conversations later, I realized that they were only word games, intellectual puzzles that aborted thought.

Sonia and Barney were among the more complex of

the 'characters'. There were others more obviously and conventionally neurotic. One of these was the Preacher, an extremely tall man who dressed in cowboy boots, riding breeches, a flannel shirt and a Stetson hat. He would stride into the cafeteria, walk up to the first people he encountered and begin to exhort them to leave the city.

'Go find yourself a home on the plains!' he would shout. 'A free place in a wide space where you won't be bothered with no taxicabs tootling their crazy horns at you, where you can cross a street and take your time – Gawd's Country!' He would orate like this on his one and only subject, the West, oblivious to the fact that no one listened, until suddenly for no visible reason he would stop talking, stare belligerently about for a moment and then stalk angrily out. I never saw him sit down at a table or join in a conversation even with the 'drifters', nor did I ever meet anyone who knew anything about him.

I would sit with these people for hours every night, afterwards going home to my sleeping room not to leave it until late in the afternoon of the next day. I cannot say I looked forward to these social hours (they were not in any way compared to the chosen leisure of a healthy man; they were only another form of my somnambulism). When I was not actually asleep, I submerged my personality in the mechanical compulsions of my job, or in an equally mechanical participation in this society of misfits. It was a complete negation of everything that had gone before.

I suppose it was inevitable that I should sleep with Sonia, although I can say honestly that at no time did I calculate it. First we fell into the habit of sitting next to each other, an accident in the beginning and then a not unpleasant institution. Later, we would walk home together in the early hours of the morning – she lived near me. During these walks we talked little, but there existed a common feeling between us which I cannot define except to say that when I was near her in this way was the closest I ever came to awaking. Then one night by mutual consent, without a word of love being spoken, we walked by her boarding house and went to my room. From then on, although it was never a constant procedure and there were many nights when she went to her place and I went to mine, we considered this a part of our relationship and I believe we both found solace in it.

One night Sonia did not come to the All-Brite and I walked home alone. This, in itself, was not unusual. Sonia often missed a night a week at the cafeteria and I never questioned her as to her whereabouts on these nights. I cannot say that I felt lonely that night either; as a matter of fact it was a beautiful night in early September, there was a blood-red harvest moon and I took a long walk along Surf Avenue, exploring all the many side streets I had never ventured down before.

Coney Island is a terrifying empty neighbourhood late at night. By two o'clock in the morning most of the concessions are closed, except for a few dance halls and bars and one merry-go-round that goes all night. A few roistering sailors staggered, yipped and brawled a short way up the street that night, the three sheets and gaudy side-show signs gleamed red in the rich moonlight, the twisted skeleton of the roller-coaster stretched its conjectural latticework up towards the pitch black sky.

I felt exhilarated, almost as if I had been drinking. I

remember I stood in front of a fun house, the façade of which featured roly-poly clowns with starchy faces and huge grinning lips, and bent double with laughter at my own crazy reflection in a distorting mirror. That, I know, was the first time I had looked into a mirror with equanimity. But the distortion of this flawed surface was so grotesque that it relieved the natural horror of my face, and by making it ridiculous enabled me for an instant to accept it. I was still laughing at the insanely contorted self I had seen, as I turned down my own street and started for my rooms.

Except for the main stem, Coney Island streets are dark at nights – and in 1944 they were doubly dark because of the blackout. Still the moon supplied a neon light of its own. I had walked this street many times and I had grown to like its ramshackle air; even the occasional rumble of the elevator seemed reassuring. Then, all of a sudden, I was afraid.

I do not know for how long I had been aware of footsteps sounding behind me, but at that moment I realized that they did not belong to a casual pedestrian but rather to someone who was following me. Trembling, I stood aside to let this person pass – sure that he would not.

When I turned around no one was there.

I was childishly panic-stricken. I experienced an irrational attack of terror. I remember that I put my hand up to my face to feel my scar, automatically, as if it were in some way connected with my phobia. I stood there for several minutes, holding my breath, feeling my heart hammer at my ribs and my blood freeze in my veins, ready to flee at the sight of a shadow or the sound of an echo. But no one came.

I started for home again.

And the sound of footsteps followed me! Whoever it was must have hidden in a doorway when I stopped and turned around. On the blacked-out street I did not discover his presence. I knew now that whoever it was intended to do me harm – why else hide? I walked fast.

The person behind me walked fast, too. I began to run. He ran. I ran as fast as I could, and by then I was only a block from my house. If I could reach my door, would I be safe? All I could hear was the sound of those feet. He seemed not ten paces behind me. Then I became aware of an automobile coming down the street towards me. I ran out into the street in front of it, waving my arms frantically to flag it down. I could see that its headlights were mere glowing slits, but I preferred the known danger of being run over to the unknown danger the footsteps implied . . .

The last person I thought of before the car hit me was Sonia. For some reason her hair was slicked back like a man's and she had a moustache. I hated her.

6

BETWEEN TWO WORLDS

There are times in anyone's life when it is possible to stand aside and see what is past, as well as what is present, with an objectivity that is unnatural if not god-like. A few minutes after I was knocked down in the street near my rooming house, I came to in what was to me then – at that moment – a strange bed in a strange room. It was a small room, clean, but cheaply furnished. The door stood partly open and through it I could see a dimly lighted hallway and a banister. Over the dresser, in the place where a mirror would normally be, several cheap reproductions of famous paintings had been thumb-tacked to the plaster: a Van Gogh, a Cézanne and a Degas. I was pleased to see them since these are my favourite painters. All this I perceived in the foggy instant between full consciousness and the depths of unconsciousness.

Then, as I struggled to awake fully, the recent past surged in on me: I felt a sharp, unyielding pain at the base of my brain, I heard again the roar of a motor racing wildly and felt the rush of wind as a bulk – huge and menacing – hurled past me, caught at me, threw me down. At this I was greatly confused. Several conflicting images appeared to my mind's eye, many faces looked down at me: one, that of a man with a moustache, another, a dwarf's face underneath a bowler hat, others I could not quite descry. Then hands lifted me, and, uncannily, it seemed as if I were lifted twice at the same time – as in a double printed motion picture you see the same action duplicated, two sets of images doing the same thing – and voices said different things, different voices! One said, 'He's dead! Get the photo, quickly!' Another cried, 'Oh, I saw it happen! Is he hurt badly? Here, let me help you. He lives only down the street – we can take him there!'

Then the struggle ended, one set of memories won out. At the same time I recognized the little man who was sitting on the foot of my bed. I was wrily dismayed. He was Eustace.

While I stared at him, I remembered that I had become frightened in the street, that I had run into the path of an automobile and that Sonia had come along right afterwards and helped to carry me down the street and upstairs to my room. But what was the other memory I had awakened with, the one that had contested unequally, for a glimmering, with the more recent past? Was I remembering what had happened in the subway station? And what was Eustace doing here? Was he the one who had been following me?

As I looked at him, I realized that I wanted badly to know the answers to these questions. Perhaps, he could tell me? If I played it right, I might learn something. The thing to do was to pretend that I was confused. I thought about it and arrived at a plan that seemed brilliant. I would act as if I had suffered another attack of amnesia I would say I had forgotten everything that had happened recently. By this tactic I would put him on the defence. And, if he had been following me with a purpose, I would find it out.

Eustace was not wearing fancy clothes this time: his suit was conservatively cut and a carefully brushed bowler hat rested on his knees. 'What are you doing here?' I asked him.

'You could have been hurt bad, chum!' he said. 'That car gave you a nasty clip. I had to come up to make sure you were all right, didn't I?'

His voice was still the same mechanical-sounding guttural, but it was not pitched sarcastically as it had been when I first heard it. In fact, he was smiling uneasily, smoothing his hat with one hand, patting his knee with the other. He was trying to be ingratiating.

'I saw you over on the Avenue,' he went on. 'I've been wanting to see you for a long time but I never expected to find a swell like you here! I've been wanting to talk to you. I followed you and you started to run. Before I could catch up with you' – he glanced down at his short legs – 'you ran out into the street in front of that jalopy.'

I rubbed my head and my hand came away bloody. I had knocked loose a hastily contrived bandage. Eustace jumped to his feet and made clucking noises with his tongue. He came over to me and helped me tie the bandage tighter.

'It's only a deep scratch,' he said, 'but you better lie still for a day or so. You can't tell, from a lick like that it might give concussion!'

I could see that my plan was working. The little man was rattled. He had not expected to find me suffering from amnesia and, now that he surmised this was the case, he did not know what to say. I was not sure that I would learn anything from questioning him, but I could at least find out what sort of a game he had been playing on Jacob. I was curious about that.

'What's he been doing? Picking at it?'

Sonia was standing in the doorway. She held a basin of water in her hands and she was smiling. Her eyes were shadowed, her hair gleamed darkly in the poor light, her slim figure was silhouetted against the brighter illumination that came from the hallway – I liked her looks. Tonight she was wearing a loose-fitting Russian blouse and flannel trousers that looked well on her long legs. I regretted that, until Eustace left, I would have to pretend that I had forgotten her.

'Why don't you introduce me to your friend, John?' she asked. 'He was very kind to wait to be sure you were all right after that awful bump you had. Particularly after the driver left you in the street like that!'

Eustace was watching me expectantly, waiting to be introduced. Sonia was regarding me solicitously. I decided to embarrass the little man as much as I could.

'This is Eustace,' I said. 'A leprechaun.'

Sonia took it calmly, only barely raising an eyebrow. 'Irish?' she asked. I could see she thought I was joking. Maybe I was.

'No, he is an American leprechaun.'

Eustace was discomfited. He squirmed. 'I been meaning to tell you about that,' he said. 'That's one of the reasons I've been wanting to see you. I want to tell you how that was.'

'What's his last name, John?' Sonia asked.

'I don't know his last name,' I said.

'It's Mather,' said Eustace. He squirmed some more.

'Eustace Mather?' She raised her eyebrow a little higher.

'No lady,' said the little man. 'My name ain't Eustace,

82

it's Felix. Felix Mather.' He looked at me unhappily. 'I've been meaning to tell you,' he said.

At this point Sonia put her arm around me. I liked that. 'You've never spoken of Felix before, John,' she said. 'Is he a friend of yours?'

'Business acquaintance, lady,' said Felix. 'Eustace was my trade name at one time.'

She pulled me to her and brushed her lips across my forehead. 'I like you, Felix,' she said to the little man. 'John should have let me meet you sooner.'

I looked at her and, though I tried hard, I could not keep from smiling. I was enjoying this game. How surprised she would be at what I was going to say next!

'Who are you?' I asked her. 'You tell me who you are first, and then I'll tell you about him.' I motioned to Felix.

Her wide mouth lost its smile and her eyes seemed to disappear completely into the shadows of her brows. Her arm dropped on to the bed – away from my shoulders. I missed the familiar pressure.

'I'm Sonia, darling. Your Sonia. Don't you really remember? Oh, what a bump you must have had!' She said this last as much to Felix as to me. I could not see the expression on her face, but I could tell from the sound of her voice that she was concerned about me. I found myself wanting to take her into my arms and assure her that I was all right. Instead, I continued to ask questions.

'But, Sonia, what am I doing here? What are you doing here?'

She gave me a frightened, non-comprehending look. But when she answered my question she spoke calmly and quietly, the way one talks to an invalid.

'You live here, John. And I live down the street. You've just had a bad fall and you're still shaken up.

Now lie down and forget about everything and when you wake up it will all have come back to you.' She began to fluff the pillows behind my head and to undo my shirt for me. She was putting me to bed.

'I don't want to go to sleep,' I said. 'I don't know where I am. I don't know who you are. Nor how I got here. I'm not even sure I know who I am!' This last was the worst fabrication of all. I knew who I was all right. I was two people: John Brown and George Matthews. But I could not let Felix-Eustace know I had been leading a double life. If he knew, and he really had something to tell about Jacob, he might get suspicious and shut up. At least, that was how I reasoned then.

Sonia finished taking off my shirt and began to undo my trousers – right in front of Felix and against my protests! She undressed me, took a pair of pyjamas out of the bureau and helped me on with them, pulled the covers about me and kissed me on the lips without saying a word. After she kissed me, she said, 'I insist that you rest now, John. You may have suffered a concussion, you know. It wouldn't be good for you to over exert yourself.'

I sat up in bed abruptly, throwing myself close against her so that she had to embrace me to keep from losing her balance. Her dark hair fell about my face and smelt strangely sweet. I kissed her again.

'You called me "John",' I said. 'That isn't my right name. My name isn't John.'

She laughed at me and laid her head on my shoulder, looking up at me, smiling. 'I won't believe that you've lost your memory to that extent! Your name is John Brown and you know it!'

Felix stared uneasily in his chair. 'No, it ain't lady,' he said. 'That's Dr George Matthews you're kissing!'

Sonia pushed herself away from me. She stared curiously at the little man.

'You're kidding,' she said. 'He's John Brown and he works nights at the All-Brite cafeteria.'

'I don't know about that, lady,' said Felix. 'I only know that when I met him his name was Matthews and he was a doctor.'

I was not too pleased with this turn in the conversation. I had planned to confuse Felix in an attempt to gain information he might not otherwise let me have – but instead of learning anything myself, Sonia was learning facts about me I would rather she did not know. And there was little I could do about it.

Sonia looked at me. She was still smiling, but her smile now seemed to say, 'You're trying to fool me, but why?'

'Are you a doctor, John? You never told me that.'

'I'm a psychiatrist,' I said. I hesitated, not knowing what to say next. Then I decided that, having gone this far, I had better try to continue the deception – until Felix left. 'What I want to know,' I continued, 'is what I am doing here? The last I remember I was having a fainting spell in the Canal Street station of the I.R.T.'

Sonia stopped smiling. 'John, to the best of my knowledge you haven't been out of Coney Island in the past month. You go to work and you come home, then you go back to work again. The only relaxation you get is after work nights at the cafeteria. Why should you go to Manhattan today? And what business would you have on Canal Street?'

From now on the game got wilder and wilder. I regretted ever having begun the gambit. But now I was in too deep. I had to continue to lie and hope I could explain away later. 'I had to see Lieutenant Anderson,' I said. 'Miss Bulkely awakened me this morning and said

Jacob was being held for the murder of Frances Raye. I was home then in my own bedroom in New Jersey. What I want to know is how I got here?'

Sonia was being motherly – and the attitude did not suit her too well. She put her hand on my forehead. 'I'm going to take your temperature. You're certainly delirious and that's a sure sign of fever.'

I put my hands on her shoulders and shook her gently. 'I am not delirious!' I said. 'Please listen and try to understand what I'm saying to you!' Then I spoke slowly and emphatically, hoping that she would see that I meant more than I said, and keep quiet. 'I don't know you, Sonia. I don't remember ever having seen you before. I've never even seen this room before!'

Felix still had his hat on his head, but instead of leaving the room he came closer to my bed. He was looking at me and I saw that his forehead was even more wrinkled than was natural. His eyes betrayed his bewilderment. Sonia was regarding me too, but at last she had nothing to say. Her dark eyes had disappeared again into the hollows of her brows and her mouth quivered slightly. She reminded me of a disappointed child who does not realize why she has been disappointed.

'Frances Raye was killed the twelfth of last October,' said Felix. He put his finger to the brim of his diminutive derby as if to apologize for mentioning this fact. 'I know because they had me up as a material witness. I was in jail three weeks. I was in the Tombs.'

Sonia looked at Felix and then back at me. She moistened her lips with her tongue, but did not try to smile. I knew that she did not know what we were talking about, but the implications frightened her.

'Frances Raye was murdered no longer ago than last night!' I contradicted Felix. 'Not more than six hours

86

after I left you with that crazy horse of yours on Third Avenue. What sort of a hoax are you trying to bring off now?'

I should not have raised my voice to the little man. He straightened up so that he seemed to have gained inches of height and his eyes became cold chips of marble. Yet, perhaps, if he got angry enough he would talk.

'You've just lost about ten months some place, chum!' he said. 'Ain't no business of mine if that's the way you want it. I came here friendly because I wanted to talk to you to explain how things were . . .' He paused and stared at me. 'Because I figured you might have been handled a little rough somewhere along the line, and maybe I knew something you oughtta know . . . and maybe you could tell me some things, too . . .' He stopped and glanced at Sonia, then shrugged his shoulders and began to move towards the door. 'But I see I'm intruding between you and the lady here . . .'

I stopped him just before he reached the door. 'Don't leave now, Eustace!' I cried, without realizing until I said it that I had called him by the name I first knew. 'I have to get straightened out somehow, don't I?'

He came back and sat down again on the chair. 'That's why I've been keeping an eye open for you all along,' he said. 'I figured there were still some things you were mixed up about.'

Sonia squeezed my arm and wrinkled her eyes at me. 'What are you two talking about? Sonia hasn't the vaguest notion!'

'I seem to have forgotten a lot of things,' I said, ignoring her question. 'Both of you will have to help me out.'

Felix and Sonia were watching me. The little man was perplexed; his mouth was straight and his forehead wrinkled. Sonia's face was expressionless. She was either dissimulating or deeply puzzled, possibly hurt. I did not know which.

'You want us to tell you? Is that it?' asked Felix.

I nodded my head.

'I'll start off,' Felix said. 'The only time I ever saw you before was on the twelfth of October, last year. A fellow named Jacob Blunt had hired me to do a crazy job for him. I was to pretend I was a leprechaun, whatever that is. He had me memorize some lines I was to say to a man I would meet that night, silly lines that made no sense. I took the job because he paid me well . . .' And he went on to tell about meeting Jacob and me in the bar on Third Avenue. He left out some of the details. He did not mention the percheron. But what he did say fitted what I remembered – all except the first part. When he had finished, I had some questions to ask.

I sat on the bed across from the chair on which he was sitting. I watched him while he talked. It was a queer feeling sitting there earnestly regarding a midget, hanging on to his words, trying to discover some key to the bewildering maze of my mysterious past. I realized with a start that the more I looked at him, the less I knew about him. In fact, the more he said, the less I knew.

'You say Jacob hired you to pretend that you were a leprechaun. Why did he do that?' I asked him.

The little man shook his head. 'Don't ask me, chum. He didn't tell me. I only worked for him.'

'Where did you meet Jacob?' I asked. 'And how did he come to hire you?'

'I answered an ad in *The Times*,' said Felix. 'Then he told me his proposition. It sounded like easy money so I agreed. All I had to do was to be at a particular bar at a particular time and say a few lines to a guy he would bring with him. That was you.'

'But what about the percheron?' I asked. 'Where did it come from?'

Felix looked blankly at me. 'What percheron?' he asked innocently.

'The big horse out in the street. The horse you told Jacob he would get twenty-five dollars for delivering to Frances Raye.'

The small man clapped his derby with his hand. 'Oh, that horse!' he said. 'Oh, I didn't have anything to do with that! Jacob supplied the horse.'

I had a feeling that Felix was pulling my leg. He was too bland about this, too eager to be helping and in helping – confuse. 'I suppose you know nothing about the flower-wearing or the whistling-at-Carnegie Hall either,' I said sarcastically.

He shook his head from side to side. 'I don't know what you're talking about,' he said.

'And neither do I!' said Sonia. 'John, you must have a fever! You're making no sense at all. Who is this Jacob you keep referring to?' Still looking at Felix, I answered her. 'Just listen now, I'll explain later.'

'What did Jacob and you have to do with the murder of Frances Raye?' I asked the little man.

Again he shook his head. 'Nothing. Nothing at all. That was an accident.'

'You mean she wasn't murdered? That she was killed accidentally?'

'No, no.' He put his pudgy hand to his forehead. 'She was killed all right, but they've never found out who did it. The accident was that they had me in jail for three weeks as a material witness thinking I knew something about the murder.'

'What happened to Jacob? Where is he?'

'He disappeared completely. I don't know where he is.'

'Then what did you do after they released you?'
I asked.

'I went back to work at Coney Island. I'm still working
here. But I've been spending my spare time looking for
you. I thought that maybe it was my fault you lost
yourself. I thought you might be in hiding. I wanted
to tell you that you were safe – that they couldn't pin
it on you.'

My mind was whirling. How much of what Felix-
Eustace was telling me was true I did not know. If Jacob
had been deluding me, what was his motive? Could it
be that Jacob had killed Frances Raye and had used me
in some way to help him with his crime? I could only
question.

Sonia was standing beside me, frowning. 'Darling,
please tell me what this is all about?'

I looked at her, for the first time really critically. She
was not a beautiful woman, but I liked the way she
looked. There was an honest strength in her features and
in her direct gaze. The mannish clothes she wore added
to the severe simplicity of her long lines, accentuated
them. I realized that few tall women could dress the
way she did, successfully. Right now her hand felt soft
on my arm, but I sensed that she could be hard if she
wanted to . . .

'Tell me what you know about me,' I said to her. Her
hand tightened on my arm. Felix stood up to go.

'Don't leave us yet, Mr Mather,' said Sonia. 'I want
you to hear this, too.' She loosened her grasp on my
arm, and stood up. She looked away from both of us.

'Your name is John Brown,' she said, as if speaking
to the wall. Her voice was quiet, self-contained. I was
afraid it was cold. 'I met you about a month ago. You
worked then, as you work now, in a cafeteria.' She
stopped, turned around, her dark eyes seemed to be

on fire as she stared at me. 'I've been sleeping with you for some time now.'

Felix made an embarrassed movement towards the door. Sonia jerked her head in his direction. 'Don't leave,' she said, 'just as the party's getting rough.'

Felix sat down – uncomfortably.

Sonia, impulsively, put her arm around me. I could feel her warmth through the thin cloth of my pyjamas. I wanted to let go, to lean back hard against her, to hold her to me. I did not want to try to think it out.

'You haven't talked to me very much,' she was saying. 'That's partly my fault, I suppose, since I haven't asked many questions. I don't believe in asking questions.'

She hesitated, looked around the room, her gaze coming to rest on Felix. He fidgeted under her inspection. Then she went on, 'A girl gets curious sometimes . . . I got curious. I saw where you had been saving money, a lot of money on your salary. I looked through your pockets. I found a slip of paper that had "City Hospital" printed on it – a slip introducing you to the manager of the cafeteria. I knew then that you had been sick . . . possibly hurt . . .' Her voice continued, a quiet voice, a soothing voice, a voice that was nice to hear in a nightmare. I stared at the cheap colour prints above the bureau, at the well-dressed midget sitting on the rickety chair fondling his derby hat. And as I stared, I had a recurrence of the feeling – the perception of two realities – that I had experienced upon first regaining consciousness a half-hour or less before. One level of my mind seemed to be dealing with the present: I was thinking about the little man, Felix Mather he had said his name was . . . a funny name . . . I had known him earlier as Eustace, a leprechaun . . . an even funnier name. But as my eyes kept wandering around the tiny, cramped room looking at the net curtains over the unwashed window, at the reflections of a street lamp on the dark, streaked glass – another aspect of reality seemed to be lurking on the fringe of my awareness, I had the feeling that something important, something that had great bearing on the here and now which I had been forgetting, lingered on the tip of my tongue. And then my sight settled on the door, focused on the calendar hanging on it, on the large prominent figures – 1944.

'. . . I knew there were many things about you that I didn't know,' the quiet voice was saying. 'I knew that you were still sick . . . I guessed that there were some things you had forgotten . . . some things you could not remember. But that made no difference. Just as it makes no difference now that I know . . . some things. I still feel the same way about you. I still love you just the same, even if I have never told you that I love you until now. Those things that you forgot . . . those things that I guess you still don't remember . . . they don't make any difference . . .'

1944 – those numbers were all I could see. From October, 1943, to August, 1944, was almost a year – ten months that were dark, at least seven that were completely lost. Time that had disappeared, that could not be retrieved and re-examined like a looking-glass from which a fragment is missing that will not reflect a full view of your face. A face? A lost mirror? My face? The memory that had been lurking just beyond the edge of recall, rushed back. A mirror? Why wasn't there a mirror in my room? Why hadn't I seen a mirror at the hospital? A child's voice taunted me with words I could not understand – I heard the voice clearly (I could see the face of the child), but I could not define their meaning. And in this confusion of previous experience, this stretto of trauma like the mingling of voices before the final cadence of a mighty fugue, I returned to the confusion that always lay awaiting me below the topmost layer of my mind.

Yet out of this welter of images, sounds, ideas, emotions, came one cogent desire that was indeed a drive, a compulsion. I wanted to look into a mirror. I had to see myself in a mirror.

'I want a mirror,' I said.

I felt Sonia drop her arm from around me. I saw Felix jump to his feet, take one step backwards. I saw Sonia watching me, looking as if she wanted to cry. 'I want a mirror,' I said again.

'You stay there,' said the girl. She went over to the bureau and opened her purse. She took a small vanity mirror from it. She looked at me for a moment, as if she had not decided what to do about my request, and then handed the small square of silvered glass to me. 'It doesn't make any difference,' she said. 'I don't want you to think that makes any difference. How many times am I going to have to tell you that I never see it any more?'

I was looking into the mirror, seeing again my face and the ripe scar, remembering my first sight of it – not too long ago – the curiosity and revulsion that had changed to apprehension and dread and then to acceptance and disgust. And now I heard again and understood the little boy's words: 'Mama, how did he get like that?'

I walked over to Felix. He stood up to meet me, but even so I had to stoop to get at him. I grabbed his throat in my hands and began to shake him back and forth. He was choking. I was wringing his neck as I might a damp rag.

'How did you know me? If you hadn't seen me since last October, how did you know me? I didn't look like that before!'

Then I felt Sonia's hand on my shoulder, and I heard Sonia's calm voice in my ear. 'Let go of him, John. You're killing him. It is not his fault, John. He had nothing to do with it. Let go of him.'

I let go of him. He lay there gasping on the floor, trying to speak. When he managed to get the words out they came in painful phrases and his voice was a thickened whisper. I could see the imprint of my fingers on the flesh of his throat. I could still feel his skin writhing under my fingers. 'I saw your back . . . it looked . . . familiar. I tried to catch up with you. But you ran away. You ran . . . ran into . . . the car. Then I saw your face, I knew it was you . . . although you looked . . . terribly different.'

Later, I apologized. He was still afraid of me and he could not get out of my place fast enough. I made him give me his address, which he did reluctantly – writing it down on a scrap of paper Sonia found. I could not think straight. I was still unreasonably angry at him. All I could see was that bright scar dividing my face. That scar should not have been there. Felix went away rubbing his throat.

I did not lose his address.

7

THE DILEMMA

'What was all that about?'

Sonia was standing with her back to the door. Felix had just left. I had sat down again on the bed. My head was aching and I did not feel well.

'I pretended that I did not know who I was to confuse him,' I said. 'I thought I might learn something about . . . about my past.'

Sonia stuck her hands deep into her trousers' pockets. 'Tell me the truth, John. Have you killed someone?'

Her question surprised me. My heart jumped beneath my ribs. Then I remembered that she knew nothing about the death of Frances Raye except what she had gathered from my conversation with Felix.

'No,' I said. 'I am not a murderer. Although it looks like I was meant to be a victim.' I began at the beginning and told her the whole story of Jacob and his 'little men', the phone call in the middle of night, the impostor I found at Centre Street, my accident in the subway and my awakening, late in May, in the psychopathic ward of the hospital. I described how I had lied my way out of the hospital and my shock at finding that I had a horrible disfigurement.

'But why did you continue to call yourself John Brown?' she asked. 'Why didn't you go at once to the police and try to locate your wife instead of—' She did not complete her sentence. Her face was expressionless, but from the way she blinked her eyes I could see that she was fighting back tears.

'How could I go back to Sara looking like . . . like this?' I asked. 'I did not look this way before, you know?' I stroked my face with my hand. 'I cannot bear to look at it myself. How could I go back to her?'

'I never see it any more!' Sonia said with quiet emotion. 'It makes no difference to me!'

'But, don't you see, I could not bear it to make a difference with . . . with Sara?'

Sonia did not answer. She turned her head away and would not look at me. I felt miserable.

We talked that night, Sonia and I. We had much to say to each other. I told her all I could remember about my past: my childhood in Indianapolis, my father's death, the years at medical school in Cincinnati and the post graduate work in psychopathology in Zurich, the hard years of the early thirties, my mother's death, my marriage and my slowly rising fortunes until I could call myself a success at thirty-six. I tried to explain why I had felt apathetic when I left the hospital, why I had continued to lead the life of John Brown instead of trying to recover the career of Dr George Matthews. 'A psychiatrist should look distinguished,' I said, 'not like a clown.' I tried to make her see why I had been unwilling to attempt to recall the happenings of my black period – the seven months between the 12 October 1943, and the last part of May 1944. But as I talked I found myself losing the very apathy I was defending, and beginning to be angry instead. Who had done this to me? What had happened and why had it happened? This left me worse off than before. As long as I allowed myself to forget the blank spots, to ignore them and live only in the present, I had no immediate problems. But now I was regaining my sense of identity, and I realized what an impossible situation I was in. I had two complete personalities, John Brown's and George Matthews'. I was Dr George Matthews to myself, but I was John Brown to Sonia and all my friends in Coney Island. When I looked into a mirror, I saw a horrible face that matched the life of John Brown, not Dr George Matthews. But it had been Matthews' face before it had been Brown's.

Sonia told me all she knew about me. There was nothing new in this. After the first shock of realization that I had a wife as well as a double personality, she adopted a sympathetic attitude to my problem. I knew that she had been hurt by the way I had acted, and I guessed that she was also afraid for my sanity – especially after I attacked Felix. But she was also in love with me.

It was Sonia who suggested the theory which I later came to think of as my 'working hypothesis'. She reminded me that I had suffered at least two accidents, one in October, 1943, and another that night. Amnesia, a mental disorder that caused me to forget my past, had certainly resulted from one – if only for a short time. When I had awakened that night after being struck by the automobile, I had forgotten the scar on my face and – for an instant – I had confused the recent past with the less-recent past. If this was true, was it not likely that I had also lost my memory regarding my past life at the time of the accident in the subway? During the seven months between my fall in the I.R.T. station and my awakening in the hospital, I had called myself John Brown, had worked and received a Social Security Card.

'Or someone – the same person who had pushed me into the train in the subway, perhaps – gave me that card,' I proposed.

'Then you think someone tried to kill you, too,' Sonia said.

We were having coffee which she prepared on the hot plate in my closet. As she said this, I suddenly realized the full extent of the injustice that had been done to me. For a long time I had been unwilling to face the fact that all these things had not just happened, but that someone had done them to me for a reason. Here I was, living in a dingy room on a counterman's wages, alienated from my wife, and I had not even made a protest!

I wanted to jump to my feet, to scream and rage. I did not do it – I have always had fairly good control over my emotions – but I could feel the anger welling up in me. Why should anyone do these things to me? 'Why should I be deprived of my profession, my home, everything of value to me including my life?' I asked Sonia.

'I don't know, John – George, I mean. I think that something like that may have happened though. Tell me, when they gave you back your clothes at the hospital, didn't they give you your wallet? And if they did, didn't it contain some identification that would have told you who you had been?'

'Only the Social Security Card with John Brown's name on it,' I said.

'But on that day last year when you had the accident in the subway, didn't you have that kind of identification on you then?'

'At that time I was carrying my membership cards in several medical and psychiatric associations, my bankbook and both my business and home addresses,' I said.

'Yet you didn't have any of these when you entered the hospital, apparently. Doesn't this point to a plot against you?'

It certainly did.

Sonia was excited. She leaned across the table and pressed my hand. 'Do you know what I think, George? I think that in that last day you must have stumbled upon some fact that was dangerous to some person or group of persons. A fact that he, or they, could not dare let you remember!'

This was what had been in the back of my mind all night, but which I had not been able to put into words.

'Why didn't they kill me then?' I asked.

Sonia shook her head. 'I think they tried – and failed. I think they might try again.'

I had nothing to say to this. It was just a supposition, of course, but an unpleasantly logical one.

'George – who is Jacob Blunt?'

'Why, I've told you,' I said. 'He was my patient. He said that "little men" hired him to do crazy things. He wanted me to help him find out if these "little men" were real.'

Sonia walked to the window. The sun was rising over the rooftops – the structure of one of the rides a few blocks away was clearly visible. We had talked all night.

'George, didn't Felix say that Jacob Blunt hired him to say certain things to you?'

'That was what he said.'

'George, don't you think you had better find Jacob Blunt?'

There was no doubt that Sonia was right. Unless I wished to give up the fight altogether, I must find Jacob Blunt. For it was inconceivable that I could return to

Sara, as I was, without some explanation of how I got this way – what had happened to me and why, who had done it. But did I want to continue the fight? And, above all else, did I want to go back to Sara and resume being Dr George Matthews?

One way I looked at it, my decision had already been made. Felix had forced it by revealing to Sonia my true identity. To the one person most important to John Brown, John Brown no longer existed. It would be difficult, if not impossible, to keep up my deception from day to day when I knew that Sonia also was aware of what I was doing. Despite myself, I was – again – Dr George Matthews.

But what about returning to Sara? I was thinking about the way I looked, the absurd, grotesque face I saw when I gazed into a glass. How had I managed to face people without feeling self-conscious? I realized that a major part of my composure during the short time I had worked at the All-Brite came from my rejection of the personality, and standards, of Dr George Matthews. George Matthews had looked a certain way – he had to or he was not George Matthews – but John Brown belonged to the vicious caricature of a face that he glimpsed in mirrors. If I went back to my old way of life, I had to overcome this feeling of wearing a disguise, of appearing to myself as another character. Of course I could persuade myself that my face looked much more vile to me than it possibly could to another. All my past training in mental hygiene supported this self-advice, but I could not believe in it. All I could see when I thought of going back was that lewd smear of outraged flesh . . . and it disgusted me. I wanted to cover my face with my hands.

I suppose the reason I decided, finally, to go back – to find Jacob Blunt – to discover what was behind everything that had happened to me (as well as what it was that had happened), was that I desired revenge. This emotion, which soon dominated me and drove me on like a cruel spur in my side, was in itself paradoxical. For I had always held that revenge was a motive alien to modern, civilized man, a primitive drive, a blood-lust that human nature had sloughed off. But the man who had cultivated this opinion – the George Matthews of a short year ago – was a different man from the George Matthews I had become; nor could the man who accepted the name today ever wholly return to the man of yesterday who had never known another.

Aware of this, I set out to recapture the past.

Sonia had to go to work and I was left alone. I decided not to go back to the cafeteria. There was no reason why I should work there – I had money in the bank and a home in New Jersey. Of course, I might not be able to get the money out of the bank without a bankbook, without identification, without resembling the man who had deposited it. And I did not want to return to New Jersey because Sara might not be there – and also because Sara might well be there.

Yet, despite my torturing ambivalence, I wanted badly to see Sara. What had happened to her in the past year? Had I forgotten her, too, when I fell in the subway? The only way to discover the answers to these questions was to go and find out. I put on my hat and coat and walked over to the elevated station. Since it was early in the morning, the huge, two-levelled structure was cavernously empty: it dwarfed me as the enormity of my task dwarfed my spirit. I tried to whistle, but the tones froze in my throat. I let three trains pass before I stepped on to one.

I got off at Wall Street and walked past Trinity Church

and down Cortlandt Street to the Hudson Tubes. In Jersey I took a bus to my neighbourhood. When I left the bus I took all the short cuts to our street, foolishly proud that I still remembered them. But when I stood in front of my house, I did not recognize it. I knew the block and the number, yet I walked past it three times before I found it. In the beginning I could not tell what was wrong – it just did not look like my house. Then I saw that it had been painted and that some of the shrubbery had been uprooted and that there was a child's tricycle on the front porch. Sara and I had no children.

I walked slowly up the steps and pushed the doorbell tentatively. Heavy steps resounded through the house. The door opened upon a large woman in an old silk dress. She had a stocking cap over her hair and a dark mole on one cheek. She stared at me aggressively.

'We don't need anything,' she said.

'I'm not selling anything.'

'Then what do you want?'

'I'd like to speak to Mrs George Matthews.'

'There's no one here by that name.'

'She used to live here I know.' I wanted to say more. I wanted to say: I own this house. Mrs Matthews is my wife! I must see her! But the words clogged my throat.

'The house was empty when we came.' The woman had begun to shut the door. 'We rented it last year. We don't know anything about the people who lived here before.'

'Who do you rent it from?' I all but shouted. I had to find out more. I could not stop now!

'The realty company rents it to us. They're still trying to sell. That's their sign out there.' She pointed to a large sign stuck into the lawn. Then she shut the door in my face.

I walked down the steps to the street and turned

around to look back at the sign. A few minutes before I had stood on the same spot and looked in the same direction, but I had not seen the sign then because I did not want to see it. How many other obvious facts had I overlooked in a similar fashion? And why did I want not to see certain things?

I looked at that sign for a long time. Then I took a piece of paper and a pencil out of my pocket and wrote down the name and address of the real estate agency: Blankenship & Co., 125 West 42nd Street, New York City.

Then I walked back to the bus stop to wait for the bus back to town.

I did not learn much at Blankenship & Co. I talked to a young man with a bland manner and eyes the colour of fish scales. He said, 'We contracted to manage Mrs Matthews' property in November of last year. We are to rent to responsible people until the opportunity presents itself to sell at a reasonable figure. The present tenants have been there since June. Are you interested in purchasing the property?'

'No,' I said. 'I'm a friend of the family who has lost touch with Mrs Matthews. I thought you might help me reach her again. Perhaps, if you told me where you send the rent money . . . ?'

When I asked this question, his fish scale eyes slid over me appraisingly. I could see he suspected my intentions. But he answered my question. 'We deposit the rent to Mrs Matthews' account in her New York bank.'

Her New York bank? Then Sara had left the city?

'Could you tell me where Mrs Matthews lives now?'

The young man stood up. 'I'm sorry, but we are instructed not to divulge Mrs Matthews' whereabouts to anyone.'

'Can't you even tell me the name of her bank?'

His mouth had compressed itself into the thinnest of lines. 'I'm sorry, but that is confidential, too.'

I took my hat and left. On the street I wondered if I would have met with more success had I told him who I was instead of saying I was 'a friend of the family'. But I could not have proven that I was Dr George Matthews. I could only prove I was John Brown.

I took a local at Times Square to Canal Street and Police Headquarters. I had decided that it was time I had a talk with Lieutenant Anderson.

The policeman at the switchboard asked me: 'Why do you want to see the Lieutenant?'

'I think I have some information about the murder of Frances Raye,' I said.

He hesitated. I could see him thinking, could tell the exact moment when he recalled the case. He did something to the switchboard, said something into the receiver strapped to his head, then looked up at me.

'Go in the second door to your right. The Lieutenant will see you shortly.'

I walked down the same corridor as I had that morning in October, 1943, but went this time to a different room. That meant the Lieutenant was not seeing me in his office. I wondered why.

I opened the frosted glass door and stepped into a brightly lighted cubicle. It contained the usual desk, three chairs, a framed map of the five boroughs of New York. I sat down on one of the stiff-backed chairs, struck a match to a cigarette and waited.

I was very nervous. Would I be able to convince the Lieutenant that I was George Matthews? We had been old friends, but would he be able to recognize me despite my disfigurement? Felix had been able to, but he had seen my back first – or so he said. It was possible that Anderson would not know me at first, and that I would have to prove my identity to him. Would he give me the information I wanted – where Sara and Jacob were – or would I have to try other means? I could advertise in newspapers. I could hire a private detective and get in touch with Sara's relatives. But I might never see my wife again. And finding Jacob promised to be even more difficult.

I do not know how long it was before Anderson came into the room. He walked over and sat down behind the desk, folded his hands on the blotter and regarded me intently. His face blenched. Then he said, 'My God! It is you isn't it, George?'

'I'm afraid I don't look quite the same, Andy.' I did not mean to speak so familiarly – while I had been waiting I had remembered the coldness of his manner at our last meeting. But I was encouraged by his easy friendliness this time. For a few moments I relaxed into the belief that everything was going to be all right.

'What has happened to you?' he asked.

'I don't know. Or, rather, I've forgotten.' I told him about meeting the man who had called himself Jacob Blunt, walking with him and Nan to the subway, falling – or being pushed? – losing consciousness.

'But, good God, George!' he said, 'when you saw the man wasn't your patient why did you take him with you? Why didn't you come and tell me?'

I did not know how to answer him. How could I explain the impulse that had misled me without reproaching him for his strangely hostile attitude toward me? I had felt then that if I could talk to the imposter in the privacy of my office, I would have been able to get him to confess his crime or implicate the real murderer. But I had to admit that I overstepped my authority, and had subsequently paid dearly for it.

'I should have told you,' I admitted. 'But, remember, I had seen the real Jacob only once, and I could not be certain that I remembered his appearance correctly.'

Anderson shook his head. 'But where have you been all this time?' he asked.

I told him about awaking in the hospital and, briefly, about my escape from the mental ward. I told him about my job in the cafeteria at Coney Island and about Sonia. I explained the apathy that had enervated me during the past month or more and how it was related to the clown-like disfigurement that had distorted my personality. At this, he clutched at a pencil and began to roll it along the blotter on his desk. 'I can well believe that,' he said. 'As you probably know, some criminologists hold that many criminal personalities can be traced to disfigurements. Scars make crimes.'

I went on to say that I had had an accident the previous night and that when I had recovered consciousness I had experienced again a momentary loss of memory. I told him of my suspicions that Felix-Eustace had been following me and related my attempts to get him to tell me more about Jacob.

When I had finished, Anderson looked up quickly. 'You think that someone tried to kill you – once, in the subway and, twice, last night. Did you get the licence of the car that struck you?'

I shook my head. 'I am not certain that another attempt was made last night. In fact, I think not. The street was dark and I ran into the car while trying to flag it down.'

'You were frightened?'

'As I said, I heard someone following me. It turned out to be Felix, and his intentions were friendly. But I did not know this at the time.'

'Why do you think they tried to kill you in the first place?'

I paused and thought before I answered. 'I think I must have stumbled upon something, learned something, that was dangerous to whoever killed Raye,' I said. 'What this could be, I don't know – unless it was the fact that I knew the man you were holding was not Jacob Blunt.'

Anderson leaned back in his chair, a tight smile on his face. 'You're being vague, you know. You say "I may have been pushed . . . perhaps, I knew something dangerous to somebody." None of that gets us any place.'

'I know I'm being vague. I can't help it. I don't remember anything else.'

The door opened behind me and another policeman came into the room. He gave Anderson a photograph that I recognized immediately as one of my own. It was one I had given to Sara!

'Where did you get that?' I asked as soon as the other policeman had left the room. 'That belongs to my wife.'

Anderson nodded his head. 'Mrs Matthews let me make a copy of this. She said it was the only existing photo of you.'

He held it up for me to see. I tried to look at it, but my mind played a trick on me. In its place I saw again the mocking travesty of a face that I had first seen reflected in the soda fountain mirror. I saw the twisted lips – one side of my mouth in a permanent laugh, the other in a fixed, downward sneer – and the livid slash that rode my nose like a sabre slash. And I felt a trickle of perspiration run down my back.

Anderson was studying the photograph. 'You'll pardon me,' he said, 'but this has been such a queer case all along that I did not want to take a chance on my memory

– even knowing you as well as I do – when identifying you. But I see now that you are the same man as this.' He tapped the photograph, then threw it on the table. I picked it up and looked at it. This time I saw it as it was: a portrait of a self I had almost forgotten, a smiling, distinguished-looking man who knew who he was and where he was and could help other people by sharing his strength.

I tried to light a cigarette, but my hand trembled too much. Anderson had to help me. I felt weak and womanish. The sense of relief, of knowing that someone at last recognized me indisputably as me, flooded my body with warmth and made a lump rise in my throat. Now I wanted to ask Anderson where Sara was, but I hesitated. I was afraid to crowd my luck. When I had mastered my emotions and looked up to see if Anderson had noticed the effect his words had had on me, I saw that he was standing with his hands clasped behind him looking at a map of the Bronx. I still did not speak. I was terrified to ask about Sara. What if she weren't all right?

Finally, Anderson said, 'That leaves us with another problem and a very cold trail.'

'What do you mean?' I asked.

He sat down and began to scratch his cheek ruminatively. 'On 18 November, 1943, a man's body was pulled out of the North River. The head had been smashed in. The body was about your build, dressed in your clothes and had your identification in its pockets. When your wife saw that body, she said it was yours.'

'That's why when Harvey Peters called you from the hospital you said I was dead,' I said.

Anderson nodded his head. 'I remember getting a call from a Dr Peters,' he said. He smiled apologetically. 'If I

108

had known then what you've told me just now, I could have saved you a lot of trouble, I suppose.'

I could see that he was blaming himself for not realizing that the body that had been found in the river wasn't mine. 'What could you do if Sara identified the body?' I said to reassure him. And then, 'I guess this means that whoever killed Frances Raye also killed this man and dressed him in my clothes?'

'It looks that way. Now we have two unsolved murders instead of one.'

'But why didn't he kill me?' I asked. 'What did happen to me? How did I get this?' I fingered my scar.

'That's what we're going to have to try to find out,' said Anderson. He bit the end off a cigar and stood up. 'And it isn't going to be easy.'

8

MEMORY OF PAIN

I had reached for my hat, thinking that the interview was over. I knew that Anderson would want to see me again, and before I left I wanted to ask him to try and get in touch with Sara for me. But I did not expect what happened next.

'It's strange that you should come to see me just now,' he said, his hand on the door. 'The Raye case has been shelved for months and there has been no new evidence – until this morning.'

He looked at me questioningly.

'Come with me to my office,' he said. 'I want you to meet someone.' He opened the door and waited for me. Then he led me down the corridor to his office.

Nan Bulkely was sitting there. She turned to look at us as we came in the door. When she saw me her eyes widened and her lips trembled. I could see her hand clutch her pocketbook. For a long moment we stared at each other, then she jerked her head away.

'Do you recognize this man, Miss Bulkely?' Anderson asked.

'Yes. He is Dr George Matthews.' Her voice was scarcely louder than a whisper.

Anderson went behind his desk and picked up a pad of paper on which he had scribbled some notes. 'This is the man to whom you referred when you gave me this deposition a few minutes ago?'

'Yes.' Again I could hardly hear her. I remained standing. What was all this about?

Anderson cleared his throat and began to read from the pad of paper he held in his hand. 'Miss Nan Bulkely, of her own free will, made the following statement in the office of Lieutenant William Anderson, Homicide Division, Police Department of the City of New York on the morning of 30 August 1944. "On Wednesday night of last week I visited Coney Island with a friend, stopped in a cafeteria for something to eat and recognized one of the employees as Dr George Matthews. This man did not see me at the time or recognize me. I knew that the police considered him dead, and that he had been involved in the murder of Frances Raye which was still unsolved. I had not seen him in nearly a year. When I first had known him he was a psychiatrist who had been treating a friend of mine, Jacob Blunt. I met him in connection with the death of Frances Raye in which Jacob was at that time implicated. You (the police) released Jacob into his custody for further questioning. I went with Dr Matthews and Jacob; after we left the police station Dr Matthews had a fainting fit in the subway and nearly fell into a train. Jacob and I took him to my apartment. Dr Matthews felt better after a short while and left, making an appointment to see Jacob in his office the next day. I thought his action was peculiar then, and I do now, since he would be held responsible for any crime Jacob might commit in the interim. But I said nothing, Jacob stayed with me for a short time and then he also left my apartment. I had not seen either Jacob or Dr Matthews again until last week when I saw Dr Matthews in the cafeteria. I barely recognized him at that time because of the terrible disfigurement he has suffered since I last saw him. His face is badly scarred, but he is obviously the same man for which the police have been searching."'

Anderson stopped reading and regarded me. 'Do you remember any of this?' he asked.

'I do not remember visiting Miss Bulkely's apartment after my accident in the subway,' I said. 'As I told you the last thing I recall is the sensation of falling – or being pushed.'

'Did you see her last week at the cafeteria?'

'I did not,' I said emphatically. I looked at Nan. She was sitting rigidly in her chair, her hands clenching the arms. Her face was pale and her eyes were wide and staring. She was badly frightened. But why? Then I remembered the way I looked, the effect the sight of my own face had had on me the first time I saw it – and I understood her fright. I looked away so she would not have to look at my face.

'Do you think I killed Frances Raye, Andy?' I asked. 'Is that what this is all about?'

Anderson sat down and began to roll a pencil between his fingers. He rolled it back and forth, back and forth. It was a while before he spoke, and during this time I kept my face turned away from Nan. 'I don't think it's impossible, but I doubt it . . . at this point. I see no motive for it. But then none of us has ever uncovered a reason for her killing. You are certainly a suspect.'

I said nothing.

'Tell me again what you have been doing since you left the hospital,' he said.

'I've been working nights at the All-Brite cafeteria and living in the neighbourhood,' I said. 'I have friends that can vouch for that.'

'But you do not remember going to Miss Bulkely's apartment or anything that happened between the time you fell in the subway and the day you woke up in the hospital – is that right?'

'That's right,' I said.

'What is your impression of Dr Matthews, Miss Bulkely?' Anderson asked Nan.

She stood up, hesitantly. She had a fur over her shoulder that fell to the floor. I started to stoop to pick it up for her – then remembered how she had reacted to my face. I turned my eyes away and let her pick it up herself. When I looked back she was regarding me. Suddenly I realized that I did not like to have her look at me either. Those staring eyes, that red hair, that beautiful, blank face – they mocked me. A memory of that same face seemed to bob along the surface of my mind like a brightly painted toy balloon floating on the surface of a pond.

She had not answered Anderson's question. I decided to forestall her. 'Jacob did not come with us that day when I took a man into my custody, Miss Bulkely,' I said. 'That man was not Jacob Blunt. I do not know who he was, but he was not Jacob Blunt.' And then I turned to Anderson. 'It seems to me that he would be your most likely suspect, not I.'

'He must be mistaken,' Nan said with surprising calm. (I had expected my statement to flurry her.) 'The man was Jacob Blunt. I knew him very well. I could not be wrong.'

Anderson kept playing with his pencil. I wished he would stop, the incessant movements of his fingers was making me nervous.

Nan adjusted her fur about her shoulders. 'I think Dr Matthews is ill,' she said to Anderson. 'He admits that he has forgotten a good deal. Isn't it possible that he has forgotten more than he realizes, and even that he is mistaken in some things that he remembers?' Anderson came around the desk and guided her to the door. I heard him say '. . . investigate his statement thoroughly, check it in every detail. We'll make certain there's no mistake. I have your address.' Then they were out in the corridor and he had shut the door on me. I was alone in the room.

And a frightening thing was happening to me. I was remembering . . . something. Something that had to do with a girl's face close to mine, her eyes watching me, something that was horrible to remember . . . that had to do with pain . . . my own pain or someone else's? I did not know.

I might be wrong. I might be remembering, even now, despite the assertions I had made, going to her apartment that day in October. Perhaps, I had gone there, perhaps, I had done other things I could not remember . . . both before and after that day.

I shut my eyes, but found I could not shut out the image of that beautiful face, those wide-open staring eyes. It would not go. And there was something else . . . something terrible that was coming that I could not prevent, that was coming again and again. And something else again, the sound of a violin . . . a sweet sound, yet horrible.

I heard the door click. I jumped to my feet, terrified. But it was only Anderson. He was smiling in his tight-lipped way.

'I telephoned the cafeteria,' he was saying. 'He says that you work there so you're probably all right. I want you to come along with me though and have the manager identify you as John Brown. Then we'll know that at least that part of your story is true.'

Anderson was still friendly – I thought that a good sign. I felt my muscles losing their tenseness. I tried to smile, but I could not. When I spoke, I stammered. 'You think I don't know what I'm saying, don't you, Andy?'

Anderson shrugged his shoulders. 'I don't think in black-and-white terms,' he said. 'Working with you taught me that, if nothing else. When you had a practice did you think of your patients as either sane or insane? You know that you didn't. They were all kinds and varieties of people and their mental aberrations differed in degree as well as in kind. You had to make up your mind about each one, independently. With a cop it's the same.

'All I have to do is to look at your face to see that something has happened to you – that you've been through a lot. But I know that your having an ugly scar doesn't mean that you murdered Frances Raye, or even that you are mistaken in your memory of what happened that day in the subway. But you do admit that you cannot remember anything after you fell in the subway. And Miss Bulkely says that you recovered consciousness quickly and then went to her apartment. This makes me want to check the other aspects of your story.'

'And it makes you curious to find out what happened during my blank months,' I said.

Anderson smiled. He stuck the pencil he had been worrying into his breast pocket pulled out a cigar and began to pick at it. 'That's right,' he said. 'And that's another reason why I want to go along with you while you retrace that part of your life that you remember. I have hopes that somewhere in the process you will begin to recall what you have forgotten. I've seen it happen before.'

I followed him out of the door and down in the elevator to the street. My thoughts were in great confusion. What was I remembering about Nan Bulkely? I could still see her face in front of mine, her burnished hair, her eyes close to mine, glittering.

I shuddered.

I watched the Lieutenant as we drove across Canal Street to the bridge and over the bridge to Brooklyn. A small, spare man with closely cropped grey hair, I had thought he looked more like a worried businessman than a detective when I first met him years ago – and I still thought so. It was difficult for me to imagine him using an automatic; my mind preferred to picture him bent over a cash register or studying a chequerboard.

He talked as he drove, giving me a short history of the Frances Raye case. 'We have never been able to follow through on a single line of reasoning from the very beginning,' he said. 'That's one of the reasons I'm taking such a personal interest in you now. You might think that I would assign this sort of routine to one of my men, send a good man out to check up on you and then read his report. Well, the reason is this: the damned business is beginning to get my goat! I don't want to make any mistakes now!'

'It's kind of you,' I said. 'I appreciate your interest.'

'Look at it from the Division's point of view,' he went on. 'Over a year ago a prominent woman was found murdered in her apartment. A drunk was caught ringing her doorbell at the same time the body was found. It looked open and shut. The newspapers created their customary hullaballoo, but we thought that all we had to do was to sit tight, ask the usual questions and make a thorough check-up and the whole thing would be sewed up and ready for the D.A. in a few days.

'What happens? I ask you, what happens? You came down, visited the prisoner, I let you have him in your custody – and then both of you disappear! We pick up a little guy who says the prisoner hired him to feed you a line, and then we have to let him go. He knows nothing, or he won't talk. We still don't find you or Blunt. We question every person we can find who ever spent five minutes with Frances Raye. No results. There is no motive, no clues, no suspects. In four solid weeks of relentless investigation we were never able to follow a solitary clue to its logical conclusions. We know less when we finished than when we started! Is it surprising that, when after all these months you show up again, I should not let you out of my sight?'

'Did you ever find Blunt?' I asked.

'He sent us a postcard last summer. I went up to see him at his place in Connecticut. It was then that I found out that the man we arrested was not Jacob Blunt. I thought we had something then and I went to work on him. He told me the same crazy story that I had heard before from you and the imposter: about being hired by this Eustace (who said his real name was Felix Mather) to deliver a horse to Raye. But he said that he decided not to go through with it and left the horse tied to the post. He went to a near-by bar and got soused – when he woke up the next morning he was in a hotel room at Atlantic City married to some blonde he had met when he was drunk. We checked his story and found it was true. By that time the newspapers were off the trail, and I saw to it that the story did not leak out. I still have a hunch that he has something to do with it, but I don't know what. Then again, if he was telling me the truth – and we could not disprove his story – someone might have been plotting against him. That's why I did not want the newspapers to get on to the story of what happened to him. I can get him any time I want him, even though he lives out-of-state now. We have had the sheriff of his town watching him for months.'

I was puzzled. 'If you knew that the man in the cell was not Jacob, why didn't you question Nan Bulkely further just now when she insisted that he was?'

'I don't want her to suspect that I did not accept her story. It is possible that she's guilty of the crime, but it is more likely that she is shielding someone. She's being followed right now and I hope she will lead us to something. I have a hunch that between you and her I'll get at whoever is behind all this.'

Anderson parked his car on the Avenue across the street from the cafeteria. He made no move to get out; instead he lighted the cigar he had been chewing all this time, and went on talking. He had obviously wanted to talk this all out to someone for a long time. 'You see, if I wanted to charge Bulkely with perjury and helping a prisoner to escape, I could have done it long ago. But what good would it have done to jail her? It would not have solved the case, and we would have shut down our one possible lead to the killer – for I think Nan is in it up to her neck. We might have sweated it out of her, and then again we might not have. All in all, now that you've shown up – and Nan re-enters the case voluntarily with a cooked-up story that doesn't fool anybody – I'm beginning to feel I've played it right. One of these days this thing is going to bust wide open!'

He took a long drag on his cigar and knocked some ashes onto the seat. 'We tried to find you, too, you know. Your wife was frantic. She gave us your picture and came down to Headquarters every day for weeks. Then, in November of last year, we found that body and she identified it as yours. I can't blame her for making a mistake. After a body's been in the river for a while even its own mother couldn't tell it! Your wife finally left town – went to Chicago to her parents.'

Then I knew where Sara was! I felt better. If she was in Chicago, she was safe and I could reach her any time. But, I realized, I did not want to reach her. As long as I knew where she was that was all that mattered. I had not yet made up my mind what to do about Sara. There was the scar . . . the way Nan had reacted to it was still fresh in my mind. No, Sara could wait. There were other matters to be attended to first.

Anderson was chewing his cigar contemplatively. 'So now we got two murders,' he said, 'but this time I'm going to hold on to you. You're not going to get lost again. I'm going to have some good man on your tail night and day.'

I looked at him in surprise. This I had not expected.

'I'm taking no chances,' he explained. He opened the car door and stretched his legs. 'Come on. Let's find out what the manager of the cafeteria knows about you.'

I followed him across the street to the All-Brite. I was still thinking about Sara, and about my scar.

When I walked into the All-Brite it seemed impossible that as short a time ago as the night before I had worked there. Everything about it was strange and unfamiliar – I was seeing it with George Matthews' eyes and not John Brown's – the long steam tables at the rear, the lurid orange walls, the jumpy fluorescent lighting. Although the details of the nights that I had spent there came flooding back to me, and I could recall the feeling that went with the place – a sort of desperate loneliness, a complete and hopeless loss of personality, a fear of being jobless – I found it devilishly hard to confront Fuller, the manager, to pump his flabby hand and look

120

down at his scrubbed-pink face and realize that he had ever represented 'authority' to me!

He sat down with us at one of the tables. He seemed surprised to see me. In fact, his first words were: 'What are doing here at this time of day? You're not on until six o'clock.'

I did not answer him. I waited for Anderson to ask the first question. He was considering Fuller thoughtfully, chewing a little on his cigar. Then he asked, 'Does this man work for you under the name of John Brown?'

Fuller glanced at me apprehensively. He had no way of knowing who Anderson was – the Lieutenant was in plain clothes – but he seemed to sense that something unusual was happening. He answered with exaggerated caution.

'He has been,' he said. 'A good worker, too. I was worried about taking him on – thought the customers might object to – to his face. Thought they might get complaints and I would hear about it. But he's worked out pretty well . . . so far. The breakage was less this month . . .'

'How did you come to hire him?' Anderson picked a flake of tobacco from his lips and flicked it onto the floor. Fuller's eyes looked down at it in disapproval. I knew he did not like to have his floor dirtied. But he did not say anything.

'The hospital recommended him. We get a lot of our help that way now. It's the times. The war is hard on the cafeteria business.'

'What hospital? And when did he start to work for you?' Anderson was annoyed with the way he had to pull information from the seedy little manager.

'City Hospital. The social service lady there. She sends them to me with a card. It's about the best way to get help these days.'

'When did he start work for you?' Anderson was being very curt. I knew how he felt.

'I couldn't say that. I have to look up my records.'

I broke in here. 'I can tell you,' I said. 'It was on the twelfth of July.' I would never forget that date. That was the day I had first looked into a mirror and discovered a bitter, demented clown.

Fuller nodded his head briskly. 'That's right. I remember now. It was during that hot spell in the second week of July. I had had another man until the week before, but he got in a fight with one of the grifters around here and he got sixty days . . .'

'Don't you know any more about him than that?' asked Anderson. I could see he was frustrated.

'Why?' asked Fuller. 'Has he gone and got himself in trouble?' He frowned his disapproval at the thought of 'trouble'.

Anderson leaned back in his chair and flipped the lapel of his coat to show his badge. 'I'm from the Homicide Division. Are you sure you don't know anything more about this guy?' I was surprised at how tough he could be when he wanted to.

Fuller stared at us both for an instant, then jumped awkwardly to his feet knocking his chair over in the process. It fell on the tile floor making a noisy clatter. A few people at other tables looked at us with curiosity.

'I knew I shouldn't have hired him!' Fuller was saying. 'I knew the customers would complain. I knew they'd hear about it. I kept telling myself that I should never have took him on!'

His voice rose higher and higher until it was a strangled squeak. His pale pink face had flushed a flower-pot red. Now he stopped in mid-protest and stared at me. He raised his arm slowly and pointed at me. 'You mean he's a murderer? You mean he's killed somebody?'

I wanted to laugh. It was not at all funny, but I wanted to laugh. The bug-eyed little man was so ridiculous. And I had once feared him. Now the whole thing was completely absurd.

Anderson was angry. 'I didn't say that!' he shouted. 'I just asked you if you knew anything more about him that you weren't telling me. If I wanted to tell you anything else I would tell you. Now answer yes or no – do you know anything else about the identity of this man?' He glared hard at Fuller.

The manager swallowed once or twice and then backed away. He actually cringed. He moistened his lips with his tongue, opened his mouth, croaked a few times, before he said, 'I'd never seen him before that day when he came here with the card from the hospital. I never heard of him before that.'

Anderson picked up his hat. 'That's all I needed to know,' he said. He motioned to me that it was time to go. I followed him to the swinging doors. Fuller was right behind me, and I turned around to face him. He looked at me, ran his tongue around his lips, still scared. I could not understand why, unless he thought his own security was threatened in some vague way.

He wanted to ask me a question. I waited patiently for him to form the words. Finally they came, 'You are coming to work tonight?'

'No,' I said. 'I don't work here any more. I'll be in Saturday to get my pay.'

He backed away, putting out his hands helplessly. 'But what am I going to do?' he asked. 'I need a man tonight. Where am I going to get one?'

And at one time I had been afraid of that man – I could remember the feeling.

* * *

Anderson was waiting for me on the sidewalk. We walked to his car together. 'Where do we go now?' I asked him.

'We go to see Miss Willows, the head social-worker at City Hospital,' he said. 'I want to find out what those people know about you.'

'Do we have to do that?' I dreaded going back to the hospital, back to the blank part of my past. I felt I was close to remembering, and I did not want to remember. Without willing it, the image of Nan's face appeared in my mind's eye again, close to me, bending over me. It seemed to bob and beckon, urging me to delve deeper. But I did not want to delve – I did not want to remember. I was afraid and, strangely, I was listening. Listening . . . but for what?

The Lieutenant nursed the car into the traffic. He began to drive east across Brooklyn towards the river. 'We have to follow up all the leads we have,' he said. 'The hospital is one of those leads. You remember being there but, as you well know, you may be forgetting something important. Perhaps, they know what happened to you, or, perhaps, after you talk to Miss Willows you will remember it yourself.'

He talked on, reasonably. I admitted to myself that he was right and that my fear was irrational. I let him take me back to the hospital.

Miss Willows was the same middle-aged fat woman with a broad face and a placid disposition that I had known before. Her hair was still caught up in a bun at the back of her neck. Looking at her I remembered with peculiar force my desperate lies of a few months before, the cleverly halting story I had told with bated breath, the moment when I had manufactured out of a tissue of fabrication the personality of John Brown that was to fit me better than I knew then.

124

Miss Willows did not seem surprised to see either Anderson or me. She looked in a filing cabinet and found a manila folder with the name 'John Brown' clearly marked on it. She waddled back to her desk – one of her legs was shorter than the other – and opened the folder and began to examine the cards with their closely written records. Her lips moved silently as she read them.

'Oh, yes, Mr Brown,' she said, after she had refreshed her memory at the file. 'He was one of our more interesting cases. A complete recovery despite a rather bad prognosis. And an excellent adjustment and reha- bilitation, if I do say so myself.'

'Just tell me what you know about this man,' said Anderson.

She glanced up, a little put out by the Lieutenant's crisp tone. Then she pursed her lips primly.

'He came here on the first of May this year, 1944. One of your men picked him up on the Bowery, wandering. He seemed to have no memory of his past life. He had had a bad concussion and a deep laceration on his head. The policeman thought he had been in a fight. He was not intoxicated.'

'This was just a few months ago?'

'In May. We put him in bed and treated him for con- cussion and shock. When he regained consciousness he had an obsession. He believed himself to be a psychia- trist – a Dr George Matthews. He was most convincing about it. He supplied us with all kinds of details about a fictitious past life, Of course, none of them were true.'

'You checked on them, of course?'

'We found them all to be quite fictitious. There was a Dr George Matthews, but he had been dead some time.'

'You say that the prognosis was unfavourable at first?'

Miss Willows smiled quickly. 'Did I say that? Well, at

first, yes. He had a persecution syndrome. He believed himself to be this Dr Matthews and he considered it unethical of us to keep him here.'

'He remembered later?'

'Oh, yes, it all came back! Occupational therapy, you know. A little rest in a quiet place, an opportunity to use one's hands. Oh, yes, it all came back, didn't it, Mr Brown?' Now she had turned her smile on me, a chaste, antiseptic grimace.

'Yes,' I said. 'It all came back.'

'Mr Brown was born in Erie, Pennsylvania,' she was reading aloud from the folder. 'He came from a large family. He joined the Army and served in the first World War. He was wounded and came back home. He had a hard time. He worked as a farm labourer, here, and on the West Coast. His wife died. He was on relief during the depression. He became an alcoholic.'

She stopped reading and pursed her lips again. 'A typical case, I'm afraid. Is he in trouble again?' She spoke right over me – as if I weren't there or, worse, as if it did not matter how I felt.

Anderson shook his head. 'We just wanted to check with you. This is all the information you have?'

Miss Willows smiled again. She felt Anderson's displeasure, but she did not know why he was displeased. She wanted to make amends. I could see she was not a bad sort.

'You might try one of the doctors, though I doubt if they know as much as I. This is the complete case history, you see. Very complete, in fact. Mr Brown was an unusually interesting case.'

Anderson thanked her and stood up to go. 'Oh, that's what we're here for,' she said cheerfully. 'Any time I can help . . .'

*　　*　　*

As soon as we were outside the door, he stopped and looked at me. 'Did any of those things ever happen to you?' he asked.

'No,' I said, 'none of them.'

'Then how did they get on her record?'

'I remember that much, I assure you. I made that all up. I told it to the doctors and to her. It was the only way I could get out, you see!'

Anderson scratched his head. 'No, I don't see,' he said.

'They wouldn't believe that I was Dr George Matthews. They checked with you, and they were told I was dead. They checked with my office, and they discovered that my office was no longer in existence. They tried to find Sara and they failed. They then decided that I had paranoid tendencies.'

'But I still don't see why you had to make all that up?'

'Because that was the only kind of history they expected me to have. They looked on me as a bum, a vagrant. I cadged that story from a hundred similar cases I have encountered in my career. I constructed it carefully so that in its every detail it would coincide with their preconceived notion of what my life history must be like, and by this means planned to persuade them that I had indeed recovered my memory. If I had persisted in telling the truth, they would have continued to believe that I was suffering from an aberration. All that I might have said would only have heaped coals upon the fire of their conviction. Every circumstance dissuaded the possibility, to their minds, that I might have been a psychiatrist. I was forced to create a complex lie and offer it to them as the reality. There was no other way out.'

'Didn't you ever doubt your own identity? By God, I know I would have been mixed up!'

'Sometimes I was a little confused about it,' I admitted. 'But where do we go from here?'

He laid his hand on my shoulder. His eyes studied me in kindly fashion. I realized that this man was my friend, that he was on my side – at least, for the time being. It was a pleasant sensation. 'I'm taking you home,' he said. 'I'll have a man on duty all night in front of your place. When you go out, speak to him so he can keep track of you. I don't want to take any chances.'

I was glad to get home. In fact the car could not take me back to Coney Island fast enough. Things were going on in my head. I wanted to lie down and be with whatever it was that was struggling to the surface of my memory. I was afraid, but I knew that sooner or later I would have to face it. Things had gone too far – someone had pushed me too far. Now was the time to remember – and then to act.

When I reached my room, I drew the shade and stretched out on the lumpy bed. This was all that was necessary. Nothing clicked; there was no sudden revelation. It was just that a part of me that had been sleeping had awakened. I remembered it all, completely, in each detail. Or, so it seemed at first.

Later I walked to the window and lifted a corner of the shade. A man was leaning against a doorway across the street. He was watching three small girls play hopscotch. I smiled to myself. That was Anderson's man. I might need him before the night was up. But right now I needed sleep. I lay down again and closed my eyes. There was no hurry now, no compulsion, I had plenty of time.

I knew who my enemies were now, even if I did not know why they were my enemies.

9

MEMORY OF PAIN II

Memories exist whole in the mind; to put them down in words demands sequence, a sense of time and space, of then and now. But when one remembers an event that belongs to the far past and relates it to another happening that belongs to yesterday, these memories exist together simultaneously – they are both, for a moment, now, not then. And so it had been with me when I stretched out on the bed in my small room, shut my eyes and with the blotting out of sight closed down upon the present, let the lost past seize me and hold me fast. I saw it whole, lived it all again – not in an hour, or even in several minutes, but in a single, incalculable instant . . .

A softly lighted room, the dusk blue against the windows, the sweet voice of a violin, a faint scent of perfume – I was alone in the room; but someone had just left it, someone a moment before had turned on the radio, someone was returning now – I could hear the steps in the hall. I fought the heavy weight of lethargy that smothered me. A pricking sensation existed on the edge of my consciousness – was it a previous feeling remembered or was I feeling it now? It did not matter and it was all-important (it seemed logical that it should be both at the same time). Everything loomed so very large: my head, the room, the beating of my heart, the intense harmonies of the violin. I could see the waves of sound, feel them breaking over me, threatening to engulf me. The wide windows darkened deeply into night; the footsteps grew nearer and nearer, their sound accumulating into a muffled loudness. It seemed as if whoever the person was who was approaching, he was taking an eternity to get to the door, to open it, to come into the room . . . an unbearable eternity. Then I heard a decisive sound, a metallic liquidness, a key turned gently in the lock. The person came in (I had been listening for so long, for forever), and I was terrified.

Now I could see who it was. It was Nan. This was her apartment. This was her living room. (I had been in this room how many days?) And I knew why she was here. It was time again for my 'treatment'.

She sat down beside me on the couch where I lay, reached out and took my hand. I turned my head away. The scent of perfume was no longer faint, it enveloped me. From the radio the thread of sweet sound was now joined by strings and woodwinds and what had been a sibilance began to swell to crescendo. It was almost dark and the outlines of the furniture blended into the long shadows thrown by the darkening window. I felt myself slipping away . . . falling.

'Won't you tell me? He can keep this up forever, you know. Neither Tony nor I want to do it, but we can't help ourselves. Why don't you tell us? Then you would never have to go again.'

I gritted my teeth and said nothing.

'I promised you that you would never have to go again. As soon as you were strong enough you could leave, go home. All you have to do is to tell us where

Jacob is. Nothing more. No one would ever need know you told. You can believe me, no one would ever need know you told.'

I could feel her fingernails biting into the back of my hand. I could feel her breath warm on my cheek. She was sitting close to me, talking quietly, earnestly. I said nothing.

'Think of how I feel. Do you think I like to take you to the doctor every night? Do you think Tony likes it? We are not murderers! Do you think we like to stand by and watch you suffer? What good does it do for you to be a hero? Why can't you tell us what we need to know, say a few little words, tell us where Jacob is? Then it would all be over.'

She waited for me to speak. She waited a long time until the room grew black dark. She turned on a light, then stood in front of me. I would not look up at her, but I could not help seeing her legs, the bottom of her skirt, the belt of her dress.

Suddenly, she knelt in front of me. Her eyes were wet. She had been biting her lip and it was bleeding. Her hair was disarrayed. Her coat was flung over her shoulders, she wore a hat. She was ready to go, to take me with her . . .

'Please, Dr Matthews . . .'

I turned my face away.

She cried quietly for a few minutes, then she went to the closet for my coat, the sunglasses, the bandage. She wrapped the yards of bandage around my face, loosely so I could breathe, leaving holes so I could see. She put the smoked glasses over the bandage and handed me the cane, helped me into my coat. Tony was waiting for us in the hall, nervously smoothing his slick black hair. The three of us went down in the elevator together. As usual, the taxi was waiting outside.

I am not a brave man. At times, when I have read of the tortures men have undergone in Spain, at Dachau and Buchenwald, I have laid down the book that told of this martyrdom. What ideal could be worth that agony? Would it not be better to tell them what they wanted to know – even if you were killed for it afterwards? Then, at least, death would come quickly.

You don't feel that way when it happens to you.

There were differences in my case, of course. I was not in Germany or Spain; I was in New York. What happened to me should not have happened. But it did.

I could not have told had I wanted to. I did not know Jacob Blunt's whereabouts. I had seen him once for a few hours. All I knew about him was what he had told me himself.

But Nan, Tony and the 'doctor' thought differently. They were certain I knew where Jacob was. And 'he' thought I knew where Jacob was. Many times Nan made it clear that 'he' gave the orders. They all feared 'him' and obeyed 'him'. I never saw 'him' – during all those weeks I never met my persecutor.

(I remembered it all now. It was all there. It took no effort to recall any part of it: the coming back to consciousness on the subway platform, Nan's solicitous questions, Tony's arm around my shoulders, the lift and pull of them both as they helped me to the taxi, the long drive to Nan's apartment on Central Park South, the falling asleep, the blackness returning as soon as I touched the sofa, the being awakened for the first of the daily catechisms . . .

'Dr Matthews! Dr Matthews! Wake up! It's Nan!'

'Yes.'

'You had an accident. You fell in the subway. But you're going to be all right.'

'Where am I?'

'In my apartment. You said you did not want to go to the hospital. I brought you here.'

I wondered at the time why I should have requested not to be taken to a hospital. But my head hurt. I could think about that later.

'Do you feel well enough to talk?'

'Yes.'

'I want you to tell me where Jacob is.'

'Jacob? Why, isn't he with you?'

'Not that Jacob. The real Jacob!'

'The last time I saw him was last night . . . with Eustace.' I did not want to talk. I was not thinking about what I was saying. I was answering her questions guilelessly.

'You haven't seen him since last night?'

'Seen whom?'

'Jacob. The real Jacob.'

'Who was that in the cell? The man who came with us? Didn't you call him Jacob, too?' I was beginning to remember, and I was becoming conscious – but too late.

'That wasn't Jacob.'

'Where is he now?'

'He's here with us. You'll see him. His name is Tony. But answer my question. Where is Jacob?'

'I don't know.'

'Are you certain?'

'Yes. I really don't know.'

Then she was silent for a long time. Then she went away.)

The doctor's office was near the Third Avenue 'El', not more than a five-minute drive from Central Park. Although I was taken there every night for I do not know how many nights, the bandages on my face and the dark glasses over my eyes prevented me from discovering the exact location. I know I had to walk up three steep flights of rickety stairs and I reasoned from this that the building was probably a tenement – once I brushed against a child's tricycle, always there were smells of cooking in the corridors. But while all these details were vague, there were others that were etched into my recently rediscovered memory with disconcerting clarity.

The room in which I found myself when they removed the bandages was of average size, but without windows. I suspected that the 'doctor's' office was part of a railroad flat. There were no chairs, no pictures – not even a framed diploma – on the dirty brown walls. Both doors were kept locked and bolted from the inside. The single piece of furniture was a chipped white enamel operating table, complete with straps. This was in the centre of the room and over it a glaring naked electric bulb hung by its cord from the ceiling. An autoclave hissed in one corner of the room beside the wash-basin. The 'doctor' was always washing the stiff lather off his hands when I entered the room.

He was a thin man with small, brown, bloodshot eyes. His apron was usually slightly soiled. What was left of his hair was ginger-coloured, but there was a large, circular bald spot on the top of his head – with kalsomine on his face he would have resembled a circus clown. I never heard him speak. He would look around at me, then point at the table. That meant that the 'treatment' was about to begin. He never hurried his wash: he took his time about smoothing and rinsing the suds from his arms, working with an automatic coordination, methodically. When he had dried himself, he would walk briskly to the table where I was lying to inspect the straps. Sometimes he would tighten one, or loosen another . . .

The first night I lay down on the table of my own free will. The next few times I fought bitterly with Tony (of the slick black hair, the bristly moustache), but each time I lost. Finally, after several nights of futile struggle, I submitted to the 'treatment' as inevitable – Tony was amazingly agile and strong and he overcame me easily. I feared and hated what happened next. I knew it for what it was and was aware that there were limits to the number of times they could do it to me without impairing my faculties, but it was useless to struggle. Even if I could break loose, where could I go? The doors were locked and there were no windows. Soon it would be over until the next time . . . the spasm only lasted a fraction of a second.

I'll say this for the devil: he knew how to make an injection. I never felt the needle – it was on me with the quickness of lightning. I would be flat on my back, the brilliant light from the bulb overhead glowing dully in my brain despite my shut eyelids. There would be a wait while he went back to the sterilizer for the hypodermic. Then I would feel his hand steadying, probing my arm . . . The dull red of the light would spin and swell with maniacal celerity to a blinding, vivid, all-encompassing sheath of white heat. My spine would writhe, my neck arch . . . (I have seen patient after patient in 'shock' . . . I have seen remarkable recoveries, too . . . but I shall never prescribe it again.) Then cool blackness would swim in.

I do not know whether I was given insulin or metrazol or one of the new compounds. I do know that I was taken to the 'doctor' every night for what seemed forever. I know that I always awakened back in Nan's apartment, awakened only to fall asleep again. I know that during the last few nights and days I was under morphine a good part of the time, otherwise I might not have stood the strain. They questioned me each day, of course, but I told them nothing. There was nothing I could tell them.

They had devised a perfect form of torture. Shock treatments left no trace, if the patient were strapped properly and the dosage regulated with care. They knew I had been a psychiatrist and they knew that they could count on my experience of the special effects of metrazol or insulin on others to add to the normal dread of the 'treatment'. They knew that I knew that if the 'treatments' were continued long enough, something would break.

It was a precisely calculated means of extracting the information 'he' thought I had. But the joke was on 'him'. I did not know where Jacob was. I could not supply the desired information even if they killed me in the attempt to get it.

It was a grim joke.

Sometimes I questioned Nan about 'him' and his motives. She would sit beside me in the afternoon, her head burnished by the slanting sun – the sun yellow in the large living room, her hair copper-gold, glinting.

'Why is Jacob so important to "him"?' I would ask.

She would look away. 'I can't answer that question, Dr Matthews.'

'Who is "he"?' I would ask.

She would walk over and turn on the radio, fiddle with the dials until she got music, soft music, she did not seem to like the more martial *allegros*.

'Why are you helping him? If it is true that you would prefer to have nothing to do with this, why do you keep it up?'

Her face would go pasty, her lips would tremble. 'I work for him.' She would come back and sit beside me. We would listen to Delius or Mozart or Schumann. Sometimes she would read. The sun would go down behind the high apartment buildings facing the Park. The sky would begin to darken. All this time I would be thinking of what was coming, planning ways of escaping, wild schemes foolish daydreams. But they were better than the reality of the night.

One of them I tried. One night, when we reached the street, I broke and ran for it. I could see dimly and then only directly in front of me because of the bandages and the dark glasses ('he' was very clever – 'he' had thought of everything). I ran desperately towards Fifth Avenue and heavy traffic. I could hear Tony running behind me, gaining on me. I saw a broad fellow in a Homburg hat in my path. He had some sort of a terrier on a leash; he must have been out walking the dog after dinner. I swerved to miss him, seeing for an instant his over-fed countenance, his porcine eyes. Then I heard Tony yell behind me 'Stop that man!' No reason given, only a peremptory command, yet the fat fool stretched out his arms. I tried to elude him, but there was too much of him to elude. I heard him gasp 'Oof!' as I hit him, yet, surprisingly, he held his ground. I suppose he thought he was being very brave – he probably related the incident to his bored wife later, exaggerating it proudly. The damn dog began to race around us excitedly, tangling my legs in his leash. Then Tony came up, thanked the man profusely, gripped my arm firmly and led me back to Nan and the waiting taxi.

137

That was on one of the first days. Later I did not have the energy or the hope.

I was never able to think effectively about my predicament. The 'treatments' every night prevented that. My waking hours were dominated by the memory of past nights and the dread of those to come. After I had undergone many 'treatments' – by that time the 'doctor' listened carefully to my heart each night before he administered the drug – the lethargy that fell on me precluded anything but fugitive imaginings, vague dreams of surcease.

One thing I did do. I memorized the furnishings and descriptive details of Nan's apartment. This was mainly an intellectual exercise, an automatic attempt to keep a disused member functioning, for I had little hope. I felt sure that eventually the 'treatments' would be carried too far – one spasm would prove too rigorous – and I would die or suffer severe brain damage. But it is difficult to kill hope. While I despaired, I looked about me, memorizing.

It was a large room with a fireplace; wide French windows opened on a terrace that overlooked the Park. Above the fireplace was a circular mirror of blued glass, on either side of it stood two figurines – a man with his hands out-stretched, reaching, a woman kneeling in the attitude of propitiation. The carpet was a neutral grey; the book-cases along two of the walls held brightly-jacketed novels. The large radio-phonograph was of blond wood . . .

I had no need to study the faces of my captors, Tony and Nan. I was confident that I would never be able to forget either of them (how misplaced my confidence was, since I was only now remembering). Tony's clothes were of good cloth, but too severely cut, the patterns too distinct, the shoulders padded. For hours on end I watched his reflection in the fireplace mirror as he stood guard by the front door or lounged in one of the chairs in the entry hall. Regularly every few minutes he would smooth his slicked hair with the back of his hand, then run his fingers over his moustache. He seldom smoked; only infrequently did he exchange more than a few monosyllabic words with Nan. They seemed unwilling companions.

Nan was unhappy. She managed to keep busy, spending her time reading, listening to the radio, preparing our food. But there were periods in each day when she would stand by the windows and look out over the Park. She never ventured out on the terrace, nor did she ever comment on the weather. She would stand quite straight, her hands at her side, barely breathing. It occurred to me that she might well be as much a prisoner as I, and that Tony might guard her as well as myself. But when I tried to get her to confide in me, she repelled me with silence. Or 'I work for him,' she would say. 'He pays me well.'

And I would curse myself for being a sentimental fool.

My escape came entirely by accident. One night the taxi we were riding in – we were bound for the 'doctor's' office – collided with a truck. The door beside me was thrown open by the force of the collision. Tony, who had been sitting beside me on the collapsible seat, and I were thrown to the sidewalk violently. I fell on top of him; his body cushioned my fall. I was not hurt; but he was badly injured, I think. His head was twisted strangely around and his eyes were staring and glassy, although he was still breathing. I did not linger to examine him closely – the circumstances were such as to make me forget the Hippocratic oath; instead I staggered as fast as I could down the crowded street towards the river. I looked back only once. A crowd had gathered around the upset vehicles and a police car had already reached the scene. I thought I saw Nan waving at me, motioning to me to go on.

But I am not sure.

10

TOTAL RECALL

The sound of the door opening brought me back to the present. Sonia came into the room. She reached up for the cord that dangled from the ceiling and pulled on the light; it had grown dark without my knowing it. Now I felt Sonia's body next to mine on the bed – her lips soothing my forehead – before my light-dazzled eyes could construe the outlines of her face, her soft, dark hair. I held her close to me.

'My poor darling,' she said. The soft stuff of her blouse whispered against my shirt. I half rose, then fell – convulsively – upon her, bore her to me. We were together many minutes under the bald brilliance of the unshaded electric bulb. Her body had the warmth of fever, while I rid myself of a cold, mechanical urge. Later, the shamelessness of the dangling light bulb seemed to mock me and I walked across the room to turn it off. Sonia lay watching me, a smile on her lips.

'Why did you do that?' she asked.

'It hurt my eyes,' I said. I sat down on the chair. The slats were cold to my flesh.

'Aren't you coming back?'

'I have come back. That's the trouble.'

'I don't understand you, John.'

It was queer sitting there on the cold chair in the blackness of the small room. I felt then that Sonia was hardly real, and that I was even less so. Although I heard her voice, I would have been only too glad if I could have persuaded myself that she did not exist . . . that my being in this room, at this time, close to her was but another part of a continuing nightmare. But I could not deny her reality. The last quarter-hour had been only too real.

'You're acting so peculiarly.' Her voice sounded hurt.

'My name isn't John,' I said. 'I told you before that my name is George Matthews.'

'I've always called you John.' Her tone was flat, subdued, a dissonance.

'I explained how that came to be,' I said. 'Perhaps, I should have told you that I still love my wife . . . that someday I hope to go back to her . . .'

Sonia did not speak. I felt I knew what she was thinking. 'Yes, I will,' I said, as if my affirmation could, once and for all, refute her unspoken denial. 'I know the way I look. I know that many things could have happened to come between us in this past year. But I'll take the chance. I tell you that she loves me. I know that she will understand . . .'

I could hear Sonia moving about on the bed. She was dressing. I went over to the bureau, knocked against the wall and scraped my shin in the dark, and found my shirt. While I was groping for my trousers (I had thrown them on the floor a short time before), Sonia spoke again.

'I'll need the light. You might as well pull it on.'

I did. She was standing beside the bed trying to button her blouse. I saw that I had torn it badly. The fabric was hanging loose from one shoulder.

142

'I'm sorry,' I said. 'I'll get you another.'

'It doesn't matter. I have others.' She walked to the closet and began to take her clothes off the hangers. When she had all her slacks and sweaters she laid them on the bed. She went over to the bureau and began to empty another drawer that contained her other things. I watched.

'Where will you go?' I asked stupidly. I had become used to her – more than that – and now I realized that I did not want her to leave.

'I have a place of my own.' She said this sharply. Then she glanced up at me. 'Surely you remember that?'

'Yes. I haven't forgotten.'

She sat down on the bed. The vari-coloured garments in her lap began to slip and fall on the floor. She made no move to pick them up. 'What's wrong with you?' she asked.

'I think I am suffering from the after-effects of prolonged insulin shock and repeated concussion,' I told her. 'That kind of shock frequently results in extended amnesiac periods. At least, I think that is what is wrong with me. I have all the characteristic symptoms.'

She put her hand to her forehead and looked away from me. 'I don't understand.'

I told her what I had remembered about Nan and the 'doctor' and his 'treatments'. I tried to tell my story quickly and not to emphasize its more terrible aspects, but even so she reacted emotionally. It was the first time I had seen her cry. 'Oh, how terrible!' she said. 'Why did they do all that to you? What was behind it all?'

'That's what I want to know,' I said. 'And that's what I intend to find out – not only "what", but also "who".'

She sat quietly. Her eyes never left mine. 'Why won't you let me help you?' she asked.

'I told you. I am married. I have a wife. This business between us can't go on.'

She hesitated before she spoke. Her eyes were still wet and some of her hair had fallen over her brow. 'That doesn't matter – you must understand what I say. Your wife, what you intend to do later – none of that matters. Only let me help you now. I don't want to leave you . . . alone.'

After Sonia had hung her clothes back in the closet and put her other things back in the bureau drawer, we sat across from each other while I told her again (she insisted on knowing every detail) the entire story of my strange experience. I began at the beginning with Jacob's appearance in my office and worked slowly forward to the accident in the taxi and my escape. There, as before, I stopped.

Sonia leaned towards me, her dark hair eclipsing her eyes. 'Can't you remember anything more? That's a lot of it, of course, but not enough to take up the time from the middle of October until the first of May.'

'There is more,' I admitted. 'Not much . . . I don't think it tells us anything.'

'Let me judge that,' she said.

I stood up and walked to the window. The street lights were out and only an occasional glimmer from a house or restaurant enabled me to descry the man who was still leaning in the doorway across the street, Anderson's man. A chill ran down my back as I remembered that he was placed there for my protection. I turned back to Sonia.

'After the accident I ran for blocks until I could run no more. By then I was in the neighbourhood of the East River. I entered the courtyard of an apartment house and sat on a bench opposite a fountain. I don't know how long I sat there. It must have been for hours. I know it was late at night when I finally got to my feet and began to walk to the other side of town. I had only one idea: to get home to Sara. It was like an obsession.'

'Sara is your wife?'

'Yes. Haven't I told you her name before?'

'If you have, I don't remember.'

'I had a very hard time getting home. I had no money. They had been thorough – they had thought of everything, even of taking my billfold away from me. I had to walk. By the time I reached the George Washington Bridge, far up on Riverside Drive, and clear across town, I was literally dead on my feet.'

'How did you get into Jersey?' Sonia asked.

'There is a bar near the approaches to the Bridge. I went in and begged. I had little success at first. I guess I was dishevelled and weary enough to look drunk. Then a man gave me a quarter and another man gave me a dime. That was enough to get home on.'

'Poor George!' I looked at Sonia, aroused by the feeling in her voice. There was no doubting the depth of her emotion. She was sincerely moved by my story – I only hoped she did not pity me.

I hurried on, embarrassed. 'I took a bus to my town,' I said. 'And then I was on my own street, walking towards my own house. Only then did I begin to wonder about the reception I would get; until then I had not realized that, since I had no way of knowing how long I had been missing, I had no way of knowing whether Sara was still my wife!'

'Did you have doubts?' Sonia was surprised.

'Only for a moment. Put yourself in my place. How would you have felt if you had gone through what I had? My experiences had been so terrible that I found it difficult to believe that they were over and done with

145

and that I would be allowed to resume a normal life. It was too much to expect that in a few minutes I would be home, kissing my wife, safe at last.'

'Then what happened?'

'I'm getting to that. I remember going up on the porch and ringing the doorbell. I remember noticing that there were lights on downstairs, although it must have been after midnight. I don't remember anyone answering the doorbell though . . .'

'Don't you know?'

'No. I can't be sure. The rest is very confused. The next thing I remember and, I believe, the last thing I remember until I recall coming to in the psychopathic ward of the hospital is a terrific, blinding pain in my head – not that I feel again the pain, but that I know that I felt such a pain. After that . . . nothing. I must have lost consciousness at that point.'

'But what happened?' Sonia had jumped to her feet. Her eyes seemed to be starting out of her head. I went to the window and lifted the blind to look for Anderson's man. The sight of him lounging in the dark doorway across the street was reassuring to me.

'I don't know what happened,' I said. 'Somebody must have hit me on the head with a blackjack or a gun butt or something equally murderous. I suppose that blow, coupled with the incessant strain and stress of the shock treatments, did me in for sure. I must have suffered a concussion in the subway, you see; amnesia often follows concussion. Amnesia also often follows metrazol or insulin injections. And severe amnesia almost invariably follows frequent head injuries. Concussion plus the repeated shock of the "treatments" plus another concussion . . . I marvel that I am alive!'

'But why would anyone try to kill you on your own

doorstep? And who would do such a thing? It couldn't have been Tony – you said he was injured badly in the auto crash.' Sonia thought for a moment, her hand at her forehead. 'Could Nan have followed you?' she asked.

I shook my head. 'Sonia, I tell you I don't know! It's only one more thing I must find out.'

We talked it all over a thousand times that night, in fact, we talked until the light began to seep under the drawn blind. I crossed to the window and saw that another detective stood in the doorway across the street, a heavier, older man than the one who had been there before. The night had fled; it seemed as if the hours had never been, yet neither of us felt tired or needed sleep. Indeed, we were both ravenous and Sonia set about at once to prepare breakfast.

With the smell of fresh coffee and bacon in my nostrils, I thought back over the tentative conclusions we had arrived at during our night-long discussion. 'Sonia,' I said, 'I am going to call out the major steps in our plan for action while you're busy there. I want you to stop me and correct me if you think of anything I've missed.'

'All right, George,' she said, 'I'm listening.'

'First of all,' I said, 'there is what I shall call the "timetable" of my amnesia. It begins when I fell or was pushed in the subway on the morning of 12 October, 1943. I then lost consciousness for a short period of time, no more than a few hours, regaining it when I awoke in Nan's apartment. From then until I escaped from the taxi and made my way home a month to six weeks later, the period of the "treatments", I must have been conscious a good part of the time. When I was struck a second time on the porch of my house, I lost consciousness for a longer period – or if I did not lose consciousness for the entire period, I did lose my ability to remember what happened then. As it is I have no memory of what happened from that instant until I awoke in the hospital – an interval of probably seven months.'

Sonia gestured with the cooking spoon she held in her hand. 'What do you suppose did happen during that time, George? Are you sure you can't remember anything?'

I shook my head. 'Not a thing. I believe that the key to the puzzle lies hidden in those lost months. Or I may have just wandered aimlessly. Remember the police report they had at the hospital said, "John Brown, homeless, picked up wandering".'

'But you must be able to remember something that happened during all that time!'

'Not necessarily. Amnesia plays queer tricks, especially amnesia that is at least partially conditioned by the use of shock therapy. When they were first learning to administer shock treatments to patients, before the improved electrical methods were perfected, I have seen schizoids return to consciousness after the spasm to find that they could not remember their names or their previous illnesses! Those patients often effected a complete recovery, except that it would be days or even months before they regained their memories. Now, however, with the refinement in technique such amnesia is only an occasional concomitant of the treatment and short-lived. But I have no assurance that the "doctor" who administered the drug in my case knew or even cared about modern methods. It was his job to make each injection as traumatic as possible to make me tell Jacob's whereabouts. He may not have known that amnesia would be the result, or he might not have cared.'

Sonia laughed abruptly. 'But you're not suffering from schizophrenia!'

'That makes little difference. It is the extreme effect the sudden shock has on the brain and nervous system that induces amnesia. Although I have never seen it used on a sane patient, I think such a patient would be just as likely to forget after extended treatment as a schizoid.'

Sonia went back to her cooking. 'I hate to think what you must have been like during those months without a home or money, not being able to remember who you were or what.'

I did not like to think of it either. It is difficult to think of oneself as being destitute, vagrant, a bum. No wonder the staff at the hospital scoffed when I claimed to be a psychiatrist: they had seen me when I was admitted and thought I was just another wandering lunatic with delusions of grandeur.

'Let's get back to the "timetable",' I suggested. 'I can't remember what happened from the moment I lost consciousness in Jersey until the day I awoke in the mental ward. We do know, roughly, how long that was. Frances Raye was murdered on 12 October, 1943. Since it must have been at least a month or six weeks after that when I escaped from the taxi and went home that would make that day sometime in the last part of November or 1 December, 1943. Then from December, 1943, until 1 May – the day I entered the hospital – is still a blank.'

'How long did you stay in the hospital?' asked Sonia.

'Until 12 July, 1944. That's a little over two months. I shall never forget the day "John Brown" walked out of that place a free man.'

Sonia smiled slowly. She finished putting the plates of bacon and eggs on the card table. 'And now it's the end

149

of August and if you don't come eat your eggs they'll get cold.'

I joined her at the table. 'The other night when I was struck by the car, the knock on my head did something again, relieved a pressure, perhaps. I believe that eventually I'll remember everything, even that long blank period. Yesterday, when I came to after my accident in the street, I was confused for an instant. It seemed as if something I had forgotten, something I have not remembered yet, was struggling to come to the surface of my mind.'

'You can't tell me what it was?' Sonia was watching me intently. A frown wrinkled her forehead.

'No. As I said it is all coming back, but in its own way, capriciously, in patches. I am still confused but ultimately everything will fit into place.'

'Then when you awakened night before last in this room, the first person you saw was that funny, little man, Mr Mather, and you thought you were awakening from your fall in the subway!'

'Only for a moment, for one perplexing instant, did I think that. But I pretended that I did not remember anything more at that time in an attempt to learn something from Felix.'

'Are you glad I was here?' she asked, not looking at me.

'Very glad,' I said.

We ate our breakfast and afterwards I helped her wash the dishes. When the room was straight again, the dishes back in place in the closet next to the hot-plate (we used the washstand for a sink), we lighted cigarettes. Sonia sat on the bed, while I sat on the one chair.

'Now what are we going to do?' she asked.

'I've decided to wait until Anderson comes,' I said. 'He promised to be around this morning. Then we'll get the facts on Frances Raye's death from him, how she was killed and under what circumstances – if possible, we'll get him to take us to the scene of the crime. Until you spoke of it last night I had never realized how incongruous it was for me to know practically nothing about the murder that seems to have gotten me into all this trouble.'

Sonia sat swinging her legs over the side of the bed. 'Yes,' she said, 'there must be some connection.'

'Then I think we should call on Eustace – I mean Felix Mather – and take Anderson along to see if we can't get him to tell more of what he knows,' I said.

'Do you think he knows more than he is saying?'

'I still don't understand how he knew me now that I have this.' I fingered my scar. 'When he first saw me I looked entirely different.'

'Perhaps not as different as you think. Anyway, that was no reason for trying to strangle the poor little fellow!' Sonia came over and put her arms around me to show that she did not mean to sound too severe. I looked up at her long, intent face. 'George,' she said, 'don't be hard on Felix. I think he was telling you the truth the other night.'

Sonia was too near me – suddenly I did not like the feeling I had when she was close to me like this, as if Sonia, not Sara, were my wife. As if Sara was over and dead like the past. 'But you should love Sara,' I told myself. 'It is not her fault that all this has happened. She will want you to be with her again. You cannot go on like this.'

I pushed Sonia away and stood up. She went over to the bed and began to smooth the covers; she was trying not to show me that I had hurt her. I walked to the window and looked out. Anderson's man was still there. 'I think we must see Felix again,' I said.

'You're probably right,' sighed Sonia. 'Only the one I'd see first would be Nan. You know what she did to you!' Her voice had risen until she was almost shouting. I realized that we were on the verge of a quarrel and I did not want to quarrel with Sonia. She was right about Nan, too. I should see her first.

I stood staring out of the window, biting my lip to keep from saying the hot words I felt compelled to say. I knew that I was being unfair to Sonia and that my desire to talk again to Felix was nothing but a hunch. I also knew that the real cause of my irritation had nothing to do with the investigation I proposed to make. If I had a friend it was Sonia, yet somehow she stood between me and Sara. Sara who was . . . well, for all I knew . . . little more than a comfortable memory.

I had been looking at nothing in particular, but all at once I realized that the man who had been on vigil across the street was no longer there. I half-turned to comment on this to Sonia when the doorbell rang. Sonia answered it.

Anderson stood outside, his mild face dour. The heavy-set man who had been on watch was directly behind him. I asked them in.

The Lieutenant walked into the room, then stopped in his tracks. He looked at Sonia and again at me. 'Bill, here, tells me that neither one of you left the building all night. Is that right?' he demanded.

Sonia answered, 'We haven't left this room.'

Anderson's shoulders drooped. He clenched his fist, then relaxed it. 'I told you yesterday that we had a mighty cold trail to work on, Doctor. Well, it's warmed up a little overnight. Nan Bulkely was found shot to death this morning.'

His usually pleasant blue eyes were boring into mine. I returned his stare. 'Where? In her apartment?' I asked, more to make a response than because I was curious; more to hide my own amazement than because I expected the place of Nan's murder to be significant.

'Her body was found on the doorstep of an apartment building on West Tenth Street five minutes after seven o'clock this morning by a milkman who was making a delivery. She had been shot through the temple with a .45 automatic equipped with a silencer that was found lying in the street a few yards away. The medical examiner has set the time of her death as occurring at any time during the previous six hours.' Anderson recited these facts rapidly and mechanically, and with a trace of disgust. He continued to stare at me so steadily that I was discomfited.

'I'm sorry to hear that,' I said. 'But we didn't have anything to do with it. Your own man will tell you . . .'

He cut me short with a wave of his hand. 'I'm not saying you had anything to do with it. I just want to know where the goddam horse came from!'

'What "goddam" horse?' I asked.

Anderson's face was a mask of exaggerated disapproval. 'A percheron, one of those big truck horses, was found tethered to the lamp post next to where the body was found. He had a feedbag tied on and a red ribbon in his mane.'

I regarded Anderson and Anderson regarded me. It was one of those looks that convey absolutely no meaning, but establish a community of disbelief. I kept thinking 'This is where I came in.'

But there was no convenient exit that led out of the movie and into the sane and sunny street.

11

THE BEGINNING OF THE END

Anderson wanted us to go with him to the scene of the crime. On the way over in his car, I realized that for some reason West Tenth Street was significant to me. I turned around and asked Sonia, who was sitting in the back seat, 'Do we know anyone who lives on West Tenth Street in Manhattan?'

Before Sonia could answer, Anderson cut in, 'If the street sounds familiar to you, the address would sound even more so. It's the same address as Frances Raye's.'

My voice showed my surprise. 'Do you mean that Nan Bulkely was killed in front of Frances Raye's house? Why that means both killings have occurred at the same address! Why?'

Anderson shook his head. 'Don't ask me why. The more I get to know of this case, the more "whys" I can think of myself.'

'But doesn't that mean that the same person must have murdered both Raye and Bulkely?' Sonia asked excitedly.

'It may indicate that,' Anderson conceded. 'Or it may mean that whoever killed Bulkely wanted us to think that she was killed by Raye's murderer.'

Bill Sommers, a fat detective, sat forward in his seat. 'You know, lady, murderers do funny things sometimes. Take this horse that keeps popping up, for instance. Now I gotta theory about that horse.'

'Yes?'

Sommers laid his large hand on Sonia's trousered knee. 'I think that horse is the most important clue we got to who done these murders,' he said. 'Only a guy with a sense of humour would think up a gag like that. The horses don't serve any useful purpose that I can see. He just thought it would be cute to tie a big horse to a lamp post every time he killed somebody.'

'Well,' said Anderson, over his shoulder, keeping his eyes on the road ahead. 'Let's hear your theory, Sommers.'

'That's it,' said the detective. 'We gotta look for a guy with a sense of humour. A funny guy. A card. That's all.'

'Huumph!' was Anderson's only comment. He kept his eyes on the street. Sommers kept his hand on Sonia's knee. She looked down at it, regarded it as she might some peculiar creature that she had just laid eyes on for the first time in her life, then gently removed it.

But Sommers had given me an idea. There was something in what he said, although that something was probably not what he had intended. In the last analysis the psychology of the murderer and of the practical joker did differ only in degree. Both were sadists, both enjoyed the pleasures of the grotesque and of inflicting pain on others. Murder might be termed the ultimate practical joke; similarly, a practical joke might be called the social form of murder.

There was little to see at the scene of the crime. Both the horse and the body had been removed. Two policemen stood talking to the superintendent of the building; Anderson approached them and joined in the talk. Sonia and I looked around at the sidewalk, the lamp post. What we expected to see, I do not know – blood, perhaps? We saw nothing. Sommers stood leaning against the fender of the police car, his hat tipped over his face to keep the morning sunshine out of his eyes. He seemed about to fall asleep.

After a few minutes, Anderson came back to us. 'I talked to the super,' he said, 'and he's going to let us into the apartment that used to be Frances Raye's. The lady who lives there now is out for a few hours.'

As we followed him into the foyer of the small apartment building, I said, 'You don't expect to discover any significant fact about Raye's murder here now, more than nine months after it happened, do you?'

Anderson jabbed the elevator button. 'You never can tell in this business. Finding that body outside this morning makes me wonder.'

'Won't you need a warrant?' Sonia asked.

'The super is taking the responsibility and I'll back him up if necessary. We won't touch anything and they'll never know the difference. A warrant would take too long.'

The elevator came and we went upstairs. Anderson opened the apartment door with the superintendent's key. It was a medium-sized flat, impeccably clean, furnished with severely modern furniture. Anderson stood in the middle of the living room and pointed at the floor. 'This is where we found Raye's body,' he said. 'She lay flat on her face. She had been stabbed in the back, but the knife was not to be found. There were no signs of struggle. The doors and windows were all unlocked, but the apartment was in order. We took fingerprints all over the place, but the only recognizable impressions we found were those of Raye herself and her maid's. Since the maid could prove that it was her day off, that got us nowhere. The only conclusion we could reach was that the murderer was a friend who had just walked in, and since she knew him she did not raise a fuss.'

I kept looking about the apartment – it fascinated me. I wandered into the bedroom and Anderson followed me. This room was finished in powder blue and one whole wall was a mirror. There was a low vanity and a chaise-longue beside the bed. Nothing else was remarkable.

We walked into the kitchen. Anderson opened the dumb-waiter and peered down the shaft. 'This is big enough for a man to get into,' he said, his voice reverberating in the empty shaft, 'but the super says he keeps it locked at both the bottom and the top. He insists that it was locked on the night of the murder, too. So whoever did it couldn't have escaped that way, not that there weren't other ways, plenty of them, that he could have used.'

I cleared my throat. 'Andy,' I said, 'I know something more about the man who pretended to be Jacob Blunt. The man you released into my custody.'

He looked at me suspiciously. 'You do?'

'Yes. He held me prisoner for many weeks. He and Nan Bulkely. His name is Tony. I began to remember it all last night . . .' And I told him about my ordeal in Nan's Central Park apartment, about the 'doctor' and his 'treatments', Tony's probable death and my escape.

When I had finished Anderson said, 'Why didn't you tell me this before?'

'I only remembered it last night.'

'Do you know when this took place?'

'Not exactly. It must have started the same day Tony

158

was released, the day after Raye's murder. But when it ended I can't tell for sure, perhaps a month or six weeks later.' I told him about my 'time-table' then.

'When you went back to Jersey after your escape, did you see anyone you knew? Somebody who could remember seeing you and help us arrive at a probable date?'

'No, I didn't.'

'Are you sure you didn't see your assailant before you were struck that night on your front porch? Haven't you any idea who it might have been who attacked you?'

'No. I'm sorry, but I did not see who it was.'

'There was someone in the house though?'

'There was a light on in the house.'

'Are you sure you didn't see your wife?'

'I tell you I saw nobody, Andy.'

Anderson sat down on the kitchen stool, pulled a cigar out of his pocket and bit off the end. Sonia, who had been in the living room, came into the kitchen. She saw the frown on Anderson's face and looked questioningly at me. 'I have just told him what I remembered last night,' I said in answer to her unspoken question.

Anderson kept silent for a long time. Finally, he looked up at me. 'You are certain you don't remember anything after you lost consciousness on the porch of your house? From then on remains a blank? You're not holding back anything?'

'That's all I remember. You see,' I said, 'I think being hit on the head served to bring on my amnesia. It might have overcome me anyway, or it might not – but with the effect of the concussion to add extra pressure, my loss of memory was certainly aggravated. I may have recovered from the actual blow in a few minutes, returning to a state of consciousness that resembled the normal, but at that time I probably could not remember my name.'

Anderson looked at his watch and stood up. 'We're not doing anything sitting here,' he said. 'Let's go back to Headquarters and see what the boys have dug up on the Bulkely murder. I had a man following her last night, you know. He says she left her building about ten minutes to one this morning. She met a man outside and then they took a taxi. My man was too busy hailing a cab himself to see what the man looked like. He followed their cab to Sheridan Square where he was stopped by a traffic light. He would have had the driver crash the light, but he saw them draw up to the kerb across the street and leave the taxi. He jumped out of the cab and followed them into a night club – there are several there, you know. But when he got inside he could not find them. Like a fool he looked all around the club before he asked the doorman where they had gone. The doorman had seen them. He said they came in, looked around at the crowd, then left. Somehow my man had missed seeing them. When he reached the street, they were nowhere in sight. And that's the kind of rotten break we've been getting all along!

'I've a hunch that whoever it was that Nan met is the one we're looking for, the one behind it all. Now, at least, we know that Bulkely had a part in your kidnapping. She may have been killed because she knew too much.'

'Don't forget that only yesterday she was in your office making a big point of having seen me in the cafeteria. There must be a reason for that stratagem,' I reminded Anderson.

Anderson nodded his head. 'That might have been an attempt to discredit anything you told me in advance.'

'If so, a pretty clumsy one. Because it tied right in with my story.'

He shook his head. 'Don't be too sure about that,' he said. 'It might have been just clumsy enough to look like the truth. I remember thinking yesterday that perhaps I was wrong in believing your story without more investigation. You had been released from a mental hospital recently – then this girl comes down with a report that she had seen you. She reminds me that you might be the one uninvestigated suspect in the Raye case, and that it might be profitable for me to look you up. When you walk in and ask to see me – Nan could not have expected that you would come so quickly – it would have been better for her if you had come the next day – it looks like you know you've been recognized and had decided you had better give yourself up before we came and got you.

'As I say, I wasn't at all sure I believed your story yesterday, and if I hadn't known you before I would not have been inclined to give you the benefit of the doubt. That's one of the reasons why I left a man outside your door last night – not only to protect you, but to watch you. Now, of course, I know you didn't kill Bulkely, but only because I know you didn't leave your house last night.'

'You think it's likely that the same person killed both Bulkely and Raye, don't you, Lieutenant?' Sonia asked.

Anderson smiled briefly. 'I'm not answering that question yet.'

We went outside to the waiting car. Sommers was still leaning against the fender, apparently more asleep than awake, but he stiffened to attention when he saw Anderson. I looked back at the apartment building as we began to move away. A woman was climbing the steps to the front door, a small, well-dressed woman.

I saw only her back, but my pulse began to pound in my throat. The woman was Sara, my wife, who was supposed to be in Chicago. I would know her anywhere. I craned my neck to stare back at her. She was fitting a key into the lock as we turned the corner and lost sight of her. Only then did I realize that Anderson had been watching me out of the tail of his eye.

'See somebody you know?' he asked casually.

'I'm not certain,' I said. I saw he was not going to let me off with that. I could lie, or I could be honest. I surprised myself by being honest. 'I guess my eyes were playing tricks on me,' I said. 'I thought I saw Sara.'

Anderson swerved the car abruptly down the next street, ignoring completely the one-way signs. 'We'll go back and see,' he said. We sped dizzily around the next corner and screamed to a stop on West Tenth Street. No one was to be seen. Anderson and I jumped out of the car and ran up the steps. Anderson rang the superintendent's bell.

'Did anyone come into the building just now?' he asked the man when he appeared.

The fellow shook his head. 'I didn't see anybody.'

Anderson glanced at the long row of doorbells. 'We could search each apartment,' he said to me, 'but we would have to get warrants for that many.'

'I wouldn't do that,' I said, having noted the hesitation in his voice. 'My eyes were playing tricks on me, I'm sure.'

He turned and started back to the car. 'Yes,' he said, 'that must be it. The last I heard of your wife she was still in Chicago staying with her parents. She said that if she ever came back to New York she would notify me.'

'I was imagining things,' I said. But as I said this, I made up my mind to come back and see for myself as soon as I could. I was certain that I had not been imagining things, but I was not sure that it would be a good idea to let Anderson know that.

We climbed back into the car and this time we went to Police Headquarters.

12

PERCHERONS DON'T COME CHEAP

Anderson's desk was piled high with reports from the various men he had working on the Bulkely slaying. Sonia and I sat down while he read his way through the pile of official-looking papers. When he finished, he spoke into the intercom on his desk: 'Tell Arnheim to report to me.'

Minutes later, a swarthy, dark-haired detective opened the door to the Lieutenant's office. He had narrow shoulders and a broad, jovial face.

Anderson spoke to him without looking up from the reports. 'You checked on that horse and its owner?'

'Yes, sir. Bide-Away Farms at Algonport, Long Island. A Mr Frank Gillespie. He rented the horse to a Miss Bulkely yesterday and delivered it to a stable on Seventh Avenue. I checked the stable, too. The horse was there from three o'clock yesterday afternoon until five o'clock this morning. It was delivered in a closed van and called for by the same van. The van belonged to Mr Gillespie. It has not returned yet although Miss Bulkely promised to have it returned last night. I reported it stolen this morning.'

Anderson snapped, 'I know all that. It's down here on your report. What I want to know is did any of your men see that van last night? Somebody must have seen it between upper Seventh Avenue and West Tenth Street!'

'I checked with all precincts, sir. No one reported it. A general alarm is out now and it may be picked up any minute. Or one of the men who is off-duty may have seen it and will report it later. Then again, it may have been noticed, but not reported because there is nothing unusual about seeing a moving van on the street, sir.'

Arnheim spoke quietly and rapidly. He had his facts well in hand. Anderson remained surly, but I could see this was his way of showing one of his men that he was pleased.

'You say here that this is the same man who sold another percheron to Miss Bulkely at the time of the Raye case,' Anderson tapped the report he held in his hand with his fingernail. 'Why didn't that come out then? Didn't we contact every horsedealer in this vicinity in an attempt to find the owner of that horse – and didn't we draw a blank on every one of them?'

Arnheim bobbed his head in agreement. 'That's right, chief – but this guy, Gillespie, admits he lied now. He says this dame, Bulkely, paid him ten grand for the previous horse. The price was so high because the horse was bought only on the condition that Gillespie asked and answered no questions. So when we came around he claimed to know from nothing.'

'How did you get him to talk this time?'

'I recognized him. He used to be in numbers before he went straight and I've seen him in the line-up again and again. He called himself by another name in those days – we got his record – and he's been up the river twice. He knew it would go hard for him if we cracked down, so he sang.'

'Promised him protection, hunh?'

Arnheim opened his eyes wide. Surprisingly, they were baby blue. 'Yeah, chief, I did. That was right, wasn't it?'

Anderson waved his hand in weak protest. 'I suppose so. You should have checked with me first, though.'

Arnheim's eyes gleamed. 'I didn't get a chance, chief. I could see this guy knew something. So I pushed him around a little.'

'How did you find him so quickly?'

'That was easy. Bide-Away Farms was printed on the nag's blanket. That was because this horse was rented, I figure. When Bulkely bought the other horse, she used her own blanket. Then we didn't have the clue.'

Anderson nodded his head. 'OK, Arnie,' he said 'that's nice work. Now I want you to trace that van. If necessary send a special squad out after it. If we find it quick enough, we may get another lead.'

When the detective had left the office, Anderson turned to me and asked, 'What do you make of that?'

'It looks like whoever is behind these killings has plenty of money,' I said. 'Ten thousand dollars for a horse! And, as far as I can see, it plays no essential part in the murder!'

'It certainly lends a grotesque touch,' Sonia commented.

That reminded me of what Bill Sommers had said about the murderer being a man with a sense of humour. I could not get that idea out of my mind. 'Just what part do you think horses play in this murder?' I asked Anderson.

He swivelled around in his chair. 'Criminals, especially

murderers, are fond of the sensational. They frequently trip themselves up by adding a useless, but melodramatic, touch to their crimes. I hope it works out that way this time.'

'Doesn't Mr Arnheim's evidence prove that both these murders are the work of the same person?' asked Sonia. Womanlike, she insisted on coming back to the same point. I smiled.

Anderson was also smiling at her. 'It proves that Nan Bulkely played a part in both of them. But we knew that much already.'

I had a thought. 'There is something else, too,' I said. 'Supposing that Sonia is right and that the same person did kill both Frances and Nan – then we know that he had less money to spend this time than before.'

'How do you figure that?'

'The first time the horse was bought, wasn't it? This time it was only rented. Doesn't that indicate something?' I asked.

Anderson smiled and shook his head. '"He" didn't buy or rent either horse. Nan Bulkely bought one, rented the other. She may have been acting as agent for someone else, possibly she was. But we still have no proof of that.'

He picked up another of the reports and, after regarding it intently for a moment, flicked the switch of the inter-communications system. 'Send Miss Hanover in,' he said into the microphone. Then he looked up at me. 'Denise Hanover was Bulkely's room-mate. When my men examined Bulkely's apartment this morning they found her there. Here, I'll read from the report: "When told of Miss Bulkely's death, Miss Hanover was hysterical. Later she said, 'I know who killed her!' She was placed in protective custody."'

I felt suddenly cold. I was remembering the previous

afternoon and Nan's attitude towards me. She had acted as if I were the guilty one. Could this Hanover girl know something about me that I did not know myself – that I had forgotten? I knew that my fears were neurotic and that they were conditioned by the extreme hardship and insecurity of the past months of my life, but they remained real enough. I put my handkerchief to my forehead to wipe the perspiration away. I saw that Sonia was concerned – she must have noticed my sudden pallor. Luckily, Anderson stood facing the door with his back to me so for once he did not see my reaction. Denise, seeming younger and prettier than ever before, walked into the room. Her eyes were red with tears.

I stood up and gave her my chair. She stared at me for a long moment before she sat down, her eyes glimmering with curiosity, her lips curling with revulsion. I knew that look well by now – it was the price I paid for showing strangers my face – and I had learned to take it.

Anderson introduced us and explained our presence as persons interested in the case. I said, 'Miss Hanover and I have met before in Jacob's apartment.' I saw that her eyes still stared at me and that they were large with hate. Her shoulders kept quivering. It was some time before she could speak.

'Nan's dead,' she said to me, 'and you killed her!'

Sonia jumped up and seized my arm. 'Are you sure of what you're saying, Miss Hanover?' Anderson asked.

'I know he killed her,' she said softly – so softly that her words were almost inaudible.

'How do you know?'

'He phoned her last night. She went right out to meet him. And I never saw her again.'

'You say Miss Bulkely received a telephone call that

caused her to go out on the night of her death. But how do you know that the call was from Dr Matthews?'

She pointed her finger at me. 'He has been calling her up and threatening her life since last January. Sometimes, always against my advice, she would go out to meet him after one of those calls. That's what she did last night.'

'But how do you know these telephone calls, including the one you say she received last night, were from Dr Matthews?' Anderson asked again.

'She told me,' said Denise. 'But I knew it without her telling me. She used to get calls from him at the theatre – that was when she was still going with him. Then she caught him out with one of the girls from the chorus, and they had a fight and she broke off. It was then he began to threaten her. Finally she was so scared of him she asked me to come to live with her. That was this spring.'

Denise was very young, even younger than I had thought the day I first met her with Nan in Jacob's apartment. She wore too much make-up. Her face was garish now, a tear-streaked mask. Her lips were trembling so that she could hardly form her words. Strangely enough I was not surprised at what she said, perhaps, because I was past being surprised.

Anderson, though, was taken aback. He shot me a quick glance, then looked down at the papers on his desk. I could see Sonia's back stiffen and her eyes harden. All the sympathy that she had been prepared to give this girl was now gone in the face of what was, to her, an outrageous lie. But she said nothing.

'Are you certain of what you're saying, Miss Hanover? To accuse a man of murder is to make a mighty serious charge, you know? You must have the evidence to back it up.' Anderson's voice was level and steady.

Instead of answering the girl began to cry again. Her head sank until it was buried in her gloved hands and her whole body shook with genuine grief. Anderson came around from behind his desk and stood helplessly beside her, patting her back clumsily. He looked to Sonia for assistance, but Sonia's eyes were cold and indifferent. Denise quieted soon though, and took the paper cup of water that the Lieutenant had fetched from the water cooler.

She dabbed at her eyes with her handkerchief, sitting up straight in her chair, her high heels caught under the bottom rung as a child might sit.

'Let's go back to the beginning, Miss Hanover,' Anderson suggested. 'You've known Miss Bulkely how long?'

'I met her in 1941 when *Nevada!* began its run. We were both in the chorus at that time. I've lived with her since March, though.'

Anderson glanced at me. 'I didn't know that Miss Bulkely was in *Nevada!*' he said. 'What part did she play?'

The girl continued as if she had not heard his question. 'I was only in the chorus. But Nan understudied the lead. I was lonely – I had just come to New York – and she was kind to me. She never changed after she became a star.'

'When did she become a star, Miss Hanover?'

'After Frances Raye died, of course – everyone knows that!'

Sonia broke in. 'But the girl who replaced Raye was Mildred Mayfair! I ought to know, I've seen *Nevada!* three times!'

Denise nodded her head. 'Mildred Mayfair was Nan's stage name. She thought it sounded more romantic.'

'Was Miss Bulkely still playing the leading rôle at

the time of her death?' I asked. I did not notice how maladroit my question was until Denise began to cry again. 'No, Nan left the cast in June. She was tired and needed a vacation. Now she'll never be able to play it again!' Her face was taut with grief.

'What happened after she became a star, Miss Hanover?' Anderson's question was put gently, but I could see that he did not intend to be halted by her continual tears.

Denise sniffed and patted her eyes with her handkerchief. 'We didn't see so much of each other for a while. Don't misunderstand me, please. It wasn't that she went upstage. Nan was always sweet to me. It was just that she didn't have so much time to herself being a star and all . . . and having so many boy-friends.'

'You say she had many men as friends. Who were they?'

Denise sniffed again. 'I'm sure I don't know. I never pried into her personal affairs.'

'But surely you must have heard her mention some of them by name?'

'Well, yes.' Denise paused. 'Right after – no, just before she became leading lady – there was Edgar. I never saw him but he was real nice to her. He gave her a mink coat and . . . and other things. She didn't like him much though.'

'Do you know his last name?'

The girl hesitated, her face blank with concentration. 'No, I don't think I ever heard his other name. But there were others I do remember. There was Jacob Blunt. She liked him. I think he was younger than Edgar. But she stopped seeing him right after she became a star. She said he might get her into trouble about Frances Raye's death.' Denise stopped, shut her mouth tightly as if she had just realized that she might have said too much – then rushed on. 'And then there was the Doctor. He started to call her up a couple of months after she became a star, about January I think. And when she wouldn't see him, he began to threaten her. He said she knew something about Frances Raye she wasn't telling. And she didn't know a thing! – not a thing, I know that! But from then on until just last night he kept after her. Sometimes she would go out to see him, although I always begged her not to, and when she came back she would be limp and bedraggled looking. She'd be so frightened. And she had reason to be frightened! Didn't he kill her?'

Denise was pointing her finger at me again.

Anderson ignored her accusation. 'When did you come to live with Miss Bulkely? Did you say this spring?'

'It was in March. That was the funniest thing!' she said. She hesitated, pulled at her gloved finger with her teeth. 'She called me up one day – right out of the blue sky! She said she was lonely and wouldn't I share her apartment with her? Would I? Well, I should say! Her with an apartment on Central Park South!' She stopped and looked at me. 'But it wasn't because she was lonely,' she said tragically. 'It was because she was scared of him!'

'Did you ever see Nan with Dr Matthews, Miss Hanover?' asked Anderson.

The girl started to speak, then stopped. She looked down at her gloved hand and picked at a loose thread. Looking up again, she flared: 'No, I didn't! But that was only becasue he was so cagey! Always meeting her some place late at night – never coming to see her backstage or at home the way a decent person would!'

'How do you know then that the person who was threatening your friend was Dr Matthews?' Anderson was quiet and reasonable.

'Because Nan told me, that's why! Because I had no wish to doubt her word!'

Anderson smiled, but shook his head. 'I admire your loyalty, Miss Hanover, but such blind, unsupported belief isn't very reliable as evidence. We know for a fact that Dr Matthews could neither have telephoned nor murdered Miss Bulkely last night. One of our men was watching him all last night. He made no telephone calls since there is no phone in his room, and he did not leave his room all night. Someone else may have been threatening your friend – someone else may have telephoned her last night – someone else certainly killed her. But it wasn't Dr Matthews.'

Denise was on the verge of tears again. 'But I tell you she was afraid. Afraid of him! I lived with her and I know!'

'Miss Hanover, would you go out to meet a man in the middle of the night if that man had been threatening your life for months?'

She shook her head.

'But that's what you say Nan did. Can't you see that she must have gone out to meet somebody else, somebody she said was Dr Matthews to keep you from knowing who she really had an appointment with?'

'But why should she lie to me?'

Her lips trembled and I thought she was about to cry again. But I was mistaken. Instead, she unhooked her heels from the rung of the chair and stood up unsteadily. The mascara about her eyes had run over her cheeks and her lipstick was badly smeared.

'Before you go, Miss Hanover, I'd like you to identify these,' Anderson said. He was holding a sheaf of letters and postcards out to her. 'One of my men found these in Miss Bulkely's desk when he searched the apartment this morning.'

Denise took them hesitantly, glanced at all of them, and handed them back quickly. 'Those are Nan's own! Why are you meddling in them?'

Anderson ignored her question. 'Are these part of the correspondence Miss Bulkely carried on with Jacob Blunt?' he asked.

Denise stood very erect and tried to look cold and dignified. 'I really wouldn't know. I never read Nan's mail.'

'But you know his name. Didn't you just say that Nan used to see him, but had stopped because she was afraid he would get her mixed up in Frances Raye's murder?'

'Yes, but—'

'But what, Miss Hanover?' There was a sharp edge to Anderson's politeness.

'But I thought she hadn't seen him since last October. She never told me that she wrote to him. I didn't know.'

'Isn't it possible that there are many things you don't know about your friend's affairs, Miss Hanover?'

'Yes, but—'

'Isn't it possible that, if Nan could carry on so lengthy a correspondence with Jacob Blunt without your knowledge, she was also deceiving you as to the identity of the person who made those threatening telephone calls?'

'I suppose so. But—'

'Then you aren't really sure just who she went out to meet, are you, Miss Hanover? You really don't know who murdered her, do you?'

'No. But that doesn't mean—'

Anderson was peremptory. He picked up one of the letters and waved it. 'You don't know anything more about this correspondence?'

Denise shook her head. 'I thought she had broken off with him.'

Anderson opened the door for her. 'I want you to remember, Miss Hanover, that Dr Matthews could not possibly have had anything to do with your friend's death. I want you to remember that he was under surveillance all last night, including the time when she was killed. I don't want you to say anything to anybody about what you've told me here. I don't want you to let anyone know you've been to see me or anyone at Police Headquarters. Keep it all to yourself. You will remember that, won't you?'

She looked up at him and fluttered her eyes. 'If you say so, Lieutenant.'

Anderson was holding the door for her. She gave him one more lingering glance that was intended to be dramatic, then swept her fur about her throat – an absurd gesture – and bounced into the hall. Anderson shut the door violently, then leaned against it. He was obviously relieved.

'What do you make of that?' he asked us.

'I'm interested to find that Nan Bulkely was Frances Raye's understudy and thus profited directly by her death. How is it that you didn't know that before?'

Anderson's face was grim. 'I should have known!' he said. 'Somebody slipped up on that one. At the time of Raye's death my men interviewed the entire cast of the show. But no report I ever saw indicated that Mildred Mayfair was Nan Bulkely.'

'That was probably because Nan did not want you to know that if she could help it.'

'Still we should have discovered it,' said Anderson.

'We all make mistakes,' said Sonia.

'Yes, but none of my men should make an error as bad as that.' He returned to his desk and jotted down a memorandum. I could see heads rolling on the Homicide Squad.

'I don't see why Nan lied to Denise about the name of the man who was threatening her,' I said. 'Why should she say it was me? Could it be that whoever was threatening said he was me as long as he confined his actions to telephone conversations? Then, when he finally made himself known to her, she was afraid to reveal his true identity and continued to pretend to Denise that it was me?' I put this explanation forward self-consciously. I was still very much aware that I had just been accused of murder.

Anderson was chewing contemplatively on his cigar. 'Then you would interpret her visit with me yesterday as an attempt to get the police to investigate the case again and in so doing uncover her real enemy?'

'Something like that,' I agreed. 'Isn't that the way a girl, afraid for her life, might act if she wanted police protection yet was unwilling to accuse the man who was threatening her? She used me as a pretext for coming to see you, for getting you to re-open the case.'

'But how did she know where you were?'

He had me stumped. I felt that if I could know the answer to that question, I would be able to lay my hands on the murderer. I said as much to Anderson, and added, 'I feel that Nan is the link to the murderer, in fact, we already have a certain amount of evidence to prove it. But I still don't see how.'

'What about those letters?' Sonia asked. 'May we see them, too?'

Anderson picked the sheaf of correspondence off his desk and handed it to Sonia. His eyes twinkled. 'Feminine curiosity or pure intellectual interest?' he asked.

I read them over her shoulder. They were all signed either 'affectionately' or 'With Love'. They seemed to be in order of receipt: the earliest dated back more than six months, but the latest was no more recent than six weeks back. If she had received any letters from Jacob since then, they were not included. I pointed this fact out to Anderson.

He nodded his head. 'I noticed that. But I don't know if it's too significant at this stage of the game. There is nothing remarkable in her corresponding with Blunt. They had been close friends before. What we must find out is whether Jacob is in any way, other than that we know already, connected with Frances Raye's death, your kidnapping or Nan's murder.'

'I should think you had better get in touch with Jacob and ask him some pointed questions. Even if he is innocent of all connections with Nan's plotting, he may be able to throw additional light on the whole affair.'

Anderson agreed. 'I telephoned the New Britain police this morning and asked them to bring him to New York. I'm expecting to hear from them any moment. He has been under surveillance ever since the Raye case was tabled, however, and I doubt if he is involved in this latest development.'

'It seems to me that you ought to have investigated Jacob Blunt much more thoroughly than you have up to now,' Sonia commented drily.

Anderson stood up, pushing his swivel chair back against the wall with a resounding bang. 'Why?' he demanded of the room. 'How can I question or hold a man when I haven't a particle of direct evidence against him? What did he do? He got drunk and assisted in tying a horse to a lamp-post. I have no definite proof that he even did that, although he admitted it. He left the scene of the crime before it occurred – again on his own word, but we have no direct evidence that he even visited the address. Before that he went to a psychiatrist

178

who was later kidnapped – again Jacob had nothing to do with the crime. A man who is suspected of murder registers in jail under his name. That's peculiar, but not criminal as far as Jacob is concerned. The only charge I could have held him on, to the best of my knowledge, is that of disorderly conduct. And with a good lawyer he could beat that!'

'But,' protested Sonia, 'looking at the whole case from the day Jacob stepped into Dr Matthews' office until today, you must admit that Jacob Blunt has a great deal to do with it. And from what Dr Matthews tells me, whoever the person was who had him held prisoner and tortured was seeking information about Jacob's whereabouts. I just can't see how you can ignore the question of Jacob Blunt!'

Sonia was walking back and forth across the room, her dark hair swinging loosely about her shoulders. She was wearing slacks and a light polo coat, and her stride, as usual, was uninhibited by skirts. Her excitement had grown while she talked to Anderson – I had never seen her as close to anger. Anderson's ire was aroused, too. He stood behind his chair, his knuckles drumming the wood, his teeth clenched. It might have been the beginning of a real row ... if the intercom had not buzzed just then. Anderson had to lean down to the microphone to answer it.

The voice of the receptionist sounded in the small office, 'A Mr Jacob Blunt to see you, Lieutenant. He says he wants to report a murder.'

Anderson collapsed in his chair. He was so astonished that he failed to respond to the loudspeaker's question. He sat still as a stone, staring at me blankly, while the mechanical voice kept repeating: 'What shall I tell him, Lieutenant? A Mr Jacob Blunt, Lieutenant, wants to report a murder. Shall I send him in?'

At last, Anderson leaned forward and flipped the switch. 'Yes, you might as well tell him to come in,' he sighed.

I think things were just a little too much for Anderson just then.

13

A KNIFE STAINED DARKLY

Jacob was surprised to see me. He stood in the doorway of Anderson's office looking just about the same as he had on the day he visited me. He stared at me with astonishment. This time there was no flower in his hair and he was not grinning. His brown suit seemed in want of a pressing and he needed a shave. But he was enough the same that I had the feeling that I had suddenly been carried back ten months into the past – that instead of this being the last day of August, 1944, it was 11 October, 1943 – and I found myself at the beginning of it all again. I guessed from Jacob's manner that he was experiencing a similar sensation.

'Come on in,' Anderson grumbled. 'Don't just stand there. It's only Dr Matthews and he is alive and well.'

Jacob shut the door behind him. 'I thought you said he was dead.'

'It turned out I was mistaken. The body we found in the river, the one his wife identified, wasn't his – obviously. But that's a long story that will keep. Tell me what you want to see me about.'

Jacob approached Anderson's desk, but he kept looking sideways at me. I knew that he was discomfited by my appearance and that he could not take his eyes off my scar. By now I should be used to this initial revulsion people felt when they looked at me, but instead I had begun to doubt if I ever would get used to it – although I had learned to stare it down. Finally, he said, 'I'm glad to see you, Doctor. You seem to always turn up when I'm in trouble.' He swallowed and then faced Anderson. 'I – I want to report the murder of Nan Bulkely,' he stammered.

Anderson's hands had been playing with a pencil on his desk. Now they went limp and the pencil rolled off onto the floor. 'How do you know about that?' he demanded. 'Who told you?'

'I – I was with her when it happened,' Jacob said. 'I ran away afterwards. I didn't kill her, but I knew you would think I had. I went and ate breakfast and I thought it all over. Then I took a walk in the park and thought about it some more. I decided to give myself up. I – I want to face – the music.'

Anderson slammed his hand down on the desk and jumped to his feet. 'I might have known when I saw that horse,' he exclaimed, 'that this guy would be mixed up in it somehow!' He turned and glowered at Jacob. 'What do you mean you didn't kill her?'

Jacob put his hand to his head. 'We were walking along West Tenth Street,' he said, 'early this morning – we had been to a night club in the Village and we wanted a little air – when I heard a silly pop. Nan grabbed at me, started to say something, then fell in a heap as if someone had tripped her. I looked around, but I didn't see anybody. I'm sure there was no one around. But I didn't do it.' He looked appealingly at Anderson.

Anderson stared at him belligerently, his mild face twisted into a frightening scowl. 'Do you expect me to believe that story?' he asked sarcastically.

Jacob smiled submissively. 'It's the truth.'

'Haven't you forgotten something?'

Jacob shook his head. 'No, that's all that happened. We were walking along, and there was this pop, and—'

Anderson walked around his desk and laid one hand on Jacob's shoulder, an almost fatherly gesture. 'Tell me, son, didn't you forget that goddam horse? Didn't you forget all about that stinking percheron?' Anderson was being nasty, but I could not blame him for his bad temper. Too many things had gone wrong in the last few hours.

But Jacob did not understand the reason for Anderson's irony. He was only puzzled. 'What percheron?' he asked. 'I didn't see a horse this time. We were walking along and I heard—'

'Yes, yes, I know!' cut in the Lieutenant. 'You heard a bang and you looked and there was Nan, dead. It's a sad story – a very sad story.'

Jacob was shaking his head in obstinate disagreement. 'It wasn't a bang, it was a pop. A sound like – like a paper bag makes when you bust it, only hollower. It was so quiet I couldn't tell where it came from.'

Anderson glared at Jacob. I knew that he was venting all the irritation and bad temper that had accumulated during the past day on this boy. Jacob had the misfortune of being the straw that broke the back of Anderson's camel. 'Why don't you let him tell his story in his own way?' I suggested.

Anderson glanced at me, then returned his glare to Jacob. 'All right,' he said. 'Begin at the beginning. Tell me what you were doing in New York, and tell me' – he reached into the pile of papers on his desk and grabbed one of Nan's letters – 'what is the meaning of this?' He shoved the letter at Jacob.

Jacob looked at the letter and handed it back. 'That's only a letter I wrote to Nan,' he said.

'But why did you write to her? I thought you told me you were married?'

Jacob ran his hand through his curly hair and looked steadily at the ceiling. 'I am,' he said. 'I'm married all right.'

'But these are love letters,' said Anderson. 'You say all kinds of silly things in them. They're enough to turn a man's stomach!'

Jacob stood stiffly, but not without dignity. His face was flushed and he was perspiring heavily. 'What difference does it make to you what kind of letters I write?' he demanded weakly. 'I'm not living with my wife any more. In fact, she's getting a divorce. But what do you care about that?'

'I care this much,' Anderson snapped. 'The woman who received these letters was murdered this morning. She had been receiving threatening telephone calls for some time. She received the last of these calls last night, about twelve-thirty. She went out to meet the person who called. You tell me that you were with her last night and that you were with her when she was shot. It looks to me like you – who wrote her ardent love letters, who were the last one to see her alive – were also the same person who made the telephone calls and finally carried out your repeated threats by killing her. And to think that now you have the brass to come into my office and try to lie your way out of your crime with the most absurd, damn-fool story I've ever heard!' Anderson slammed his fist down on his desk knocking papers in all directions. 'Well,' he snorted, 'you may fool the Doctor, but you aren't fooling me!'

Jacob looked dazed. He hesitated, then he said in that

worried tone I knew so well, 'I didn't call Nan up last night. I met her outside the apartment building.'

Anderson continued to stare belligerently at him. 'Go on, Jacob,' I said. 'Tell us what happened.'

Jacob's eyes rolled nervously, his face twitched. Anderson had frightened him badly and it was a moment before he could speak. 'I decided yesterday to come to town for a few days. My wife had just left me for good – we never did get along, and now I know I never should have married her – and I felt like being alone and getting good and drunk. So I gave the sheriff's man you had watching me the slip and came on into town.

'I had been writing Nan off and on for the past year. Recently she had stopped answering my letters, why I don't know. I thought I might drop around to her place and see if she wanted to go night-clubbing with me. As my taxi stopped in front of her building, I saw her coming out of the apartment door. She saw me about the same time and she rushed up to me and threw her arms around me. She was very excited about something, in fact, as I held her I could feel her tremble. She said, "Oh, Jakey, I'm so glad to see you! Take me some place quick!"'

'Did she say why she was glad to see you?' I asked. Anderson was leaning back against his desk pretending not to listen to what Jacob was saying. He had a you-can-go-on-with-this-if-you-want-to-but-I've-made-up-my-mind expression on his face. 'Or did she say why she wanted you to take her some place quickly?'

Jacob nodded his head. 'As soon as we were in the taxi I asked her what was wrong. She said she had just had a fight with Denise and that she was so disgusted she did not want to think about anything. I didn't think she was telling me the truth, but I couldn't say so. "Take me some place where there is music and dancing, Jakey," she said. I felt sure she wasn't telling me all that was wrong. But I didn't feel like quibbling just then. I let her lean back against my shoulder and I told the driver to take us to this place I knew in the Village. I had troubles of my own I wanted to forget, too.'

'Then what happened?' I asked.

'There isn't much else to tell,' Jacob showed me that bashful grin of his for the first time since he had come into Anderson's office. 'We did what you would expect us to – we got drunk. Nan was sick and I took her outside for some fresh air. We sat in the park for a while, and then I suggested we take a walk. We were walking along West Tenth Street when it happened. I just heard this pop and I felt Nan grab at me and then she fell over in a scrambled heap. At first I thought somebody had pushed her . . .'

'What time was it when you left the night club?'

'It was closing time, around four o'clock.'

'And how long did you sit in the park?'

'I don't know for sure. I was pretty drunk you see. It was still dark when we left.'

'Make a guess.'

'I don't know. Maybe an hour, maybe longer.'

'Then it was probably between five and six o'clock when you were walking along West Tenth Street?'

Jacob nodded his head, but he looked dubious.

'And you didn't see anyone on the street when the shot was fired? Did you notice which direction the sound seemed to come from?'

'No. All I heard was a pop, and then I was too busy trying to help Nan to look around. When I did look around, I saw no one. The pop didn't sound too close, though. It wasn't loud enough to startle me.'

I could not think of any more questions to ask. I believed Jacob's story just as I had believed his story when he had come into my office that day so long ago. But I could see where Anderson would never believe it.

'Are you through?' Anderson asked me.

I nodded my head.

Anderson pushed the buzzer on his desk. We waited until Sommers, the fat detective, came into the office. Then Anderson pointed at Jacob, 'Take this man downstairs and see if you can get him to talk. Book him on suspicion of murder, but see that he gives you a statement first. I'll be down to talk to him later.'

Jacob started to protest, then thought better of it. But he looked at Anderson for a long time before he turned and followed Sommers to the door. As he was going out the door he turned around again, and this time he decided to speak.

'I didn't see a horse,' he said falteringly. 'I didn't see a horse all night.' Then he went out the door.

Sonia and I left Centre Street a few minutes later. I promised to report to Anderson the next morning – by then he would be through with his questioning of Jacob. We went up to the Village and had lunch at a sidewalk café. While we ate I told her about seeing Sara enter the building on West Tenth Street and about my intention of returning there to see if I couldn't find her. I explained that I wanted to do this alone, but asked Sonia to meet me at West Tenth Street in a couple of hours. Sonia said she would pass the time at a movie.

We parted and I walked through Washington Square to Fifth Avenue. It was one of those wonderful, clear sunny summer days when everyone seems glad to be alive. Washington Square was crowded with students, families and Fifth Avenue buses. The dogs were out in full force: pomeranians, schnauzers, greyhounds, cockers, collies, terriers of every sort and a few more weird breeds I could not name. Even the stately façades of the Fifth Avenue apartment building seemed warm and friendly, instead of cold and majestic.

But when I came to the building on West Tenth Street that we had visited that morning all my good feeling vanished. As I gazed at the long rows of mailboxes, each equipped with its own doorbell, I felt faint and weary. None of the names on the boxes was Matthews. How would I know which apartment Sara lived in? I could ring them all, but that would create a disturbance. I could ask the superintendent, describe Sara to him; but he would certainly recognize me and report the conversation to Anderson. I stood undecided, not knowing what to do.

And I began to think of my face. I saw again the first glimpse I had had of my disfigurement in the drugstore mirror; my flesh began to creep as I visualized that livid slash that divided my features, made my mouth twist into a permanent sneer. I put my hand to my cheek, feeling the smoothness of it, and imagined the look of revulsion that would come over Sara's face when she saw me. My stomach felt empty and a great weight pressed upon my chest. I was about to turn away . . .

Then I heard the door click behind me. I looked around and found myself face to face with Sara. She was smiling at me . . . she knew me . . . she seemed to accept me as I was. She was the same, unless she was a little more wonderful than I remembered. I looked at her for a long moment, afraid to speak as if in speaking I might break the magic – and then she gave a little gasp and fell into my arms. We held each other close like two kids in love. 'George,' she whispered in my ear. 'I'm so glad I've found you!'

I held her tighter, but I did not speak. I knew I did not need to tell Sara how miserable I had been. There was so much to tell, enough for days, and these first few moments of reunion were precious. But if I did not speak, I nevertheless communicated my emotions to her: I could feel her trembling in my arms. 'Oh, George,' she sighed, 'I was afraid I might never see you again . . .'

We went up in the elevator to her apartment and into a small living room. This room seemed strangely familiar to me. While she took off her hat and coat, I wandered around wondering at this sense of familiarity, so similar to the feeling I had had that morning in the apartment on the floor above. When Sara came back into the room I asked her, 'Why did you take a flat in the same building as Frances Raye's?'

She seemed puzzled by my question. 'Why, that was your idea, George – don't you remember? You wanted an apartment in the building because you wanted to be on the scene of the crime. You felt it was a safe place to carry on your investigation – a place where they would never look for you.'

I sat down beside her. 'Sara, I've forgotten so many things.' For the next ten minutes I told her briefly all that I remembered in just the way I had remembered it. I told her I could remember nothing from the time I was attacked in New Jersey until I came back to my senses in the hospital. 'And now you say I was carrying on an investigation,' I concluded. 'If I was I know nothing about it now.'

When I had finished Sara put her arms around me and held me close to her. I kissed her brown hair, her up-tilted nose, marvelled at the way she wrinkled her eyes when she smiled. 'George,' she said, 'you were right here in this apartment with me all that time you can't remember. We came here after you had me rent the house in Jersey. You were terribly sick from the wound in your cheek, and you wanted no one to know where you were. You would sit in the dark and tremble at the slightest noise.'

In my joy at finding her again, I had forgotten my fear that Sara would recoil from the scar on my face. Now I was amazed to discover that she knew about it already. I asked her to tell me what had happened.

She went over to a secretary and took a long box and a small notebook from the bottom drawer. She handed them both to me, then sat down on the floor at my feet, her legs crossed under her skirt the way she always used to sit, and told me the story of my blank months. 'I was frightened the first week of your disappearance last October,' she said. 'I visited Lieutenant Anderson every day to see if he had news of you. All he could tell me was that you had left his office with Jacob and that girl – later you were to tell me that the man was not Jacob but an impostor – and that Nan had told the Lieutenant that you had left her apartment after falling in the subway and refusing medical assistance.

'All through October I heard nothing of you. I was worried sick, I didn't know if you'd been killed, or if you had suffered amnesia. Then, about 10 November, one night as I was packing to leave on a visit to my parents in Chicago, the front doorbell rang.'

'You say this was on 10 November?' I asked.

'Yes. I threw the porch light on and answered the door. At first all I saw was what looked like a bundle of old clothes slumped on the porch. I also heard a rustling noise in the yard, as if a small boy were running away. But I did not see who it was. By that time, I had recognized the bundle as you and I had seen that you

190

were unconscious and bleeding profusely from an ugly wound in your face.'

Then my 'time-table' was off! The time I had spent at Nan's apartment was less than a month, instead of a month to six weeks.

Sara was pointing to the long box she had given me a few minutes before. 'Open it,' she said, 'and look at what is in it.' I opened the box cautiously. Inside was a thick layer of cotton-wool which I unwrapped. I saw a long, horn-handled hunting knife. The part of the cotton that had rested next to the blade of the knife was stained darkly with dried blood. As I looked at the wicked implement I felt the scar on my face begin to burn and all the hate that had been pent-up during the many months of my half-life repossessed my brain. I threw the box that contained the dagger aside.

'George,' Sara was saying, 'someone had thrown that knife at you! I found it buried in the lintel. Whoever threw it meant to kill you, George. Instead the knife struck you an awful, glancing blow and ripped half your face open!

'When you came to you told me about Nan and the "doctor" and the "treatments". You told me that you wanted to find the person responsible for Frances Raye's death, your kidnapping and the repeated attempts on your life, yourself – that you felt that you should be the one to bring the murderer to justice.'

I realized suddenly that I had not suffered a loss of memory at the time I was struck on the porch. This meant that another, later blow caused the amnesia, and by chance I forgot what had happened when I came to on the porch! But when had I suffered the second, later blow? I felt as if this knowledge were on the tip of my tongue, that in a few minutes I would be able to say it.

'I tried to dissuade you,' Sara went on. 'It seemed to me that you had suffered enough and that it was dangerous for you to try to hunt down the killer. But you wouldn't listen to me. You had me rent the house in New Jersey and assign an agent to manage it. You even had the agent deposit the rent monthly in our bank, and to send his reports to my parents' address in Chicago where they were forwarded to us in New York! I rented this apartment, in this building, on your theory that it was the safest place to carry on the investigation unobserved because it was the last place the murderer would expect to find you. But, beyond that, when Anderson asked me to look at a body that had been found in the North River wearing your clothes – you had been dressed in an old pair of pants and a torn shirt that were not yours when I found you on the porch – you had me identify the body as you to throw even Anderson off your track!'

'But whose body was that which Anderson found in the river?' I asked.

'From the description I gave you at the time you decided it was Tony's – the man who had guarded you, who had posed as Jacob and who must have died of injuries received in the taxi accident.'

I nodded my head. It all began to fit together, although there were still many questions to be answered. And, as Sara recounted these buried details of my past, I remembered things, too. There had been a notebook that I had kept . . . a notebook in which I had put down all my findings during my investigation. I asked Sara about it.

'You're holding it in your lap, George,' she said. 'I gave it to you a little while ago when I gave you the knife. Remember, you hired the Ace Detective Agency to do most of your work for you. They interviewed

Nan Bulkely and later her room-mate, Denise Hanover. From them you found out that Nan had been receiving threatening telephone calls which she said you made. You knew that you did not make those calls. I think you decided that if you could discover the identity of the person who was threatening Nan, you would have a clue to the murderer.'

I looked at the fat notebook in my hands. Here was documentary evidence about the blank months of my life. At last the past was on the verge of being recaptured! 'How long did I carry on this investigation?' I asked Sara.

Sara paled. She knelt and pressed my hands next to her breast so that the notebook fell on the floor. 'Oh, George, promise me you won't take up the investigation again. Please, promise me that!'

'It's out of my hands now,' I told her. 'Anderson has re-opened the investigation.' And I told her about the events of the last few days and of Nan Bulkely's death that morning. 'But answer my question. How long did I carry on the investigation?'

Sara stood up. She walked away from me. 'Until the last of April of this year, George. One day you went out on one of your rare trips – you know you very seldom left the house but let the detective agency do most of the actual spadework for you – and I never saw you again until this afternoon.'

'But where did I go that day?' I asked. 'And what happened to me?'

Her answer was amazing. 'I don't know what happened to you – apparently whatever it was caused you to lose your memory – but I know where you said you were going. It was an address in Coney Island. You'll find it in the notebook.'

*   *   *

For the next half-hour I read hurriedly through the notebook, my 'dossier' as Sara called it. The whole first section was devoted to newspaper clippings and these provided a history of the police investigation of Frances Raye's murder, most of which I already knew. I noticed that one of the tabloids had used the murder as a point of departure for a seething editorial on the inefficiency of the Police Department – small wonder Anderson was so concerned over the case!

After the many news stories came reports of what I had done from day to day. These began in late January. From them I saw that the investigation had proved slow and arduous and I had progressed little at first. As I read, I began to remember this period of my life – sometimes fragments of days would return to me before I read my curt précis of them, sometimes afterwards. I remembered the decision I made to confide in a private detective agency, and the fears that I had then that my activities would be reported to the police. But after the reports from the Ace Detective Agency began to come in, the investigation began to go forward again.

The agency had concentrated on Nan Bulkely. I had had them interview her after I had attended a performance of the long-time hit show *Nevada!* and discovered that its star, Mildred Mayfair, was Nan. One report told of a 'mysterious admirer' who had been sending anonymous gifts and making queer telephone calls. Another told of the gift of a fur coat accompanied by a card. I had pasted the card to a leaf of the notebook – how the detectives I hired managed to secure it I never knew, probably by bribery or theft. It contained only the scrawled initials: E.A.B.

On 15 March, the Ace Detective Agency had reported: 'Mayfair went out with E.A.B. after last night's performance. At the matinée today she was visibly nervous and frightened.' Later, 'Mayfair has asked Hanover to share her Central Park apartment.' This was the last of the detective agency's reports.

The next entry, and the next to last, was a long account written in my own hand of a visit I paid to a famous law firm on Board Street. As I looked at this I remembered that interview. I had spoken to a Mr James G. McGillicuddy, an ancient barrister of Scotch descent, who had served as attorney for John Blunt's estate. His answers to my questions, all concerning the estate, had been especially guarded but he had admitted that there had been 'another bequest made by Mr Blunt that was not part of his will'. I had not been able to garner much more information on this point. Some person, or persons – Mr McGillicuddy's wording was too cautious to reveal which – had been fortunate enough to be the beneficiary of a sizeable living trust fund which had been established during old Blunt's life. I could not get the name of his beneficiary and by the terms of the trust agreement it was not a matter of court record. I stressed the fact that I was Jacob Blunt's psychiatrist and needed this information for my patient's peace of mind. 'I have heard rumours about the younger Mr Blunt which, if true, do his father's memory a disservice,' the old lawyer had said with an air of chill dignity. Then he had stood up behind his fine old colonial desk and had dismissed me with a wave of the hand and an exaggerated nod of the head that might, under more favourable circumstances, have developed into a courtly bow.

But it was the last entry in the notebook that brought memories rushing back into my mind helter-skelter, head over heels. This was nothing new. It was the photograph of Jacob's childhood friend, 'Pruney', which he had handed me that first day in my office and that I had never returned to him. As I looked at it I remembered that black moment in the subway as the train rushed past me hurling me down, and I heard Nan's voice say: 'Get the photograph!' And I remembered stepping out of the elevated station at Coney Island and looking around me. Then there were many snatches of memory, images and sounds, that were not orderly or related to one another. One was a feeling of walking down a long, twisting passage and listening to a high tittering voice mock me. Another was of just one word, the word 'ocean'; I saw it in blinding letters before my mind's eye. And then, for some queer reason, I remembered the night I had stood outside the Fun House at Coney Island and stared laughing at my crazily distorted image in the flawed mirror . . .

I felt that it was all there, that in just a moment I would understand . . . I looked down at the picture in the notebook, examined the desperate face of the small boy standing beside Jacob. I saw that the picture was pasted down only at one end and that it could be lifted up. I lifted it and saw the same initials again, this time in old Blunt's handwriting as Jacob had told me when he gave me the picture – E.A.B. But there was something else, too. I had written under those initials the name, Edgar Augustus Blunt, and the address, 5755 Ocean Avenue.

It all came back to me. I remembered every detail of my expedition that day I disappeared: the second visit to the lawyer's office when I had told him honestly what I wanted and why and he had surprised me by giving me the name and address of John Blunt's mysterious beneficiary. And I remembered going to 5755 Ocean Avenue. And I knew who killed Frances Raye and Nan Bulkely.

* * *

I laid down the notebook and looked up expecting to see Sara. At first I didn't see her, although I noticed that the door to the hall was open. I smiled to myself – had I been so intent on reading the notebook that I had made Sara restless? I called, 'Sara, Sara! Where are you?' She did not answer.

I stood up to walk to the door to see if she was out in the hall. As I crossed the room I found her body stretched out where she had fallen against the sofa. She had been stabbed to death with a knife just like the one that had been thrown at me.

I picked her body up and laid it on the sofa. I bent down and kissed her gently on the forehead. I stayed there, my lips brushing the still-warm cheek. My grief was dry-eyed, perceptionless, embittered. I felt as if my life-blood had run out with hers.

Then something snapped inside me.

EPILOGUE

I

My hands will-lessly wrenched the blade from Sara's body, held it high for an instant, then threw it to the farthest corner of the room. My voice cursed. My glands poured sweat from my pores; I felt it cold and trickling. Tears purged my cheeks. Yet inside I was numb, more asleep than awake – somnambulistic.

Finally I straightened up and retreated to the chair that faced the sofa. I sat on it heavily, my gaze still riveted to Sara's body, my breathing slow and stentorian. How long it was before I lifted my eyes and looked around the room again I do not know. All I remember is that when I looked at the open door to the hall, Lieutenant Anderson was standing there.

I did not recognize him. I saw only a middle-aged man with greying hair and a sober expression. My first reaction was to be angry at this intrusion and to order the man out of my apartment. But I did not act on this impulse. A lethargy weighed on me and I sat staring

199

at the man in the door. Then I saw that he was not alone, but that there were others behind him. I saw Jacob and Sonia. At this moment, Anderson stepped into the room, and walked over to the sofa to bend over my wife's body. I had the uncanny sensation that I was watching myself, seeing my own recent actions relived. I wanted it to stop as I felt I could not bear to watch this parody. 'Sara is dead,' I said.

Anderson turned and regarded me. His eyes were cold. 'I know,' he said. 'Why did you do it?'

Sonia and Jacob had come into the room. Sonia started towards me as Anderson spoke, but an abrupt gesture of his hand stopped her. 'Why did you kill her?' he repeated.

His question had no effect on my emotions. The split continued: one part of me heard his query, considered it, responded ('I did not kill her,' I heard myself saying); while a second part of me ignored the words, did not even hear the sound of his voice, saw no intruders, remained intact and lonely.

'Then why did you call the police a few minutes ago and say, "I want to report that I have murdered my wife, Sara Matthews"?'

'But I didn't,' I said. My answer was matter of fact, a direct response to a direct stimulus. Reason did not enter into it. My mind was numb.

'Someone did. Someone made that statement, then gave this address.'

'I made no call,' I said. 'I did not kill her.'

Anderson went over and picked up the blood-stained knife. He held it carefully in a handkerchief and held it out to me. 'You killed her with this,' he said. 'Then you threw it in a corner. I think we'll find that the fingerprints on it belong to you.'

'I was reading,' I said. 'I must have been concentrating

since I heard nothing. I don't know how it happened, but it did. The door to the hall must have been ajar. Someone must have thrown a knife through it and killed her. There was no sound. I think it was meant for me.'

'You say "someone". Who?'

'I don't know. The same person who killed Frances Raye and Nan Bulkely.'

Anderson shook his head. 'I think that person is you. Oh, you've been very clever, Dr Matthews, both bold and clever. If I had been you I would never have had the courage to come to the police and enlist their aid before I committed two more murders. And it almost worked. You recognized the fact that the best sort of alibi for a murderer is a psychological set of the detective's which causes him to ignore the possibility of the murderer's guilt and to seek the culprit elsewhere. I've thought it over since last night and I can see that the story you told me about your amnesia, your persecution, your experiences in the hospital, all these things were carefully calculated to render me incapable of conceiving you as the killer.

'I followed this line of reasoning and investigated further. I found that Detective Sommers was guilty of gross carelessness. He was not on duty all the time outside your house last night. When he started his shift he had not eaten breakfast and he sneaked off to an all-night restaurant. He now admits to having been off duty between five and six this morning, the very time Jacob Blunt gives as the approximate hour of Bulkely's death. Since it was early in the morning when traffic is at low ebb, you could easily have left your place, taken a taxi to West Tenth Street, shot Bulkely and returned before Sommers got back.'

Sonia protested. 'But I was with him all that time. He never left the room!'

Anderson turned to her. 'I have only your word for that. You are his friend, and probably his accomplice.'

I listened to what Anderson had to say with unnatural calm. This could not be happening to me, and even if it was – what did it matter? Sara was dead, murdered. That was all that mattered.

But Sonia was not willing to give up so easily. 'You're bluffing, Anderson!' She was standing very straight, her shoulders thrown back, her dark eyes glowering. 'You can't prove this and you know it! If George is the murderer, where is his motive?'

Anderson smiled confidently. 'I was coming to that,' he said to her. Then he looked back at me. 'You didn't succeed in 'disappearing' last year as well as you thought. I knew your every move from the time you rented this apartment until I finally lost track of you last April. You did some peculiar things during those months. You hired a detective agency, interviewed a lot of people. You may have had an accident of some kind as you say, but it made you forget your whole past life, not just the immediate past. I had a man watching you day and night and I know. I had a man on duty here when you had your wife rent the apartment under an assumed name. That's how I knew where you were. I knew you visited Mr McGillicuddy, an old gentleman who was trustee of John Blunt's estate – I visited him, too. What I did not know from having you watched all the time, I learned from this—'

Anderson picked the notebook up from where I had thrown it on the floor. 'This apartment was searched thoroughly one week-end recently when your wife was away. I had photostats made of the leaves of this notebook.' He picked up the knife. 'There was another knife just like this one in the apartment then and it had your fingerprints on it.' He looked at it, then back at the body, saw that there were two identical knives in the room. 'Why, this is it!' he exclaimed. 'And I think we'll find it is the knife you used to kill Raye just as that one was used to kill your wife.'

He laid down the notebook and pointed to it dramatically. 'This alone contains all the circumstantial evidence we need to convict you. It's a very complete record of a man in search of his past. Oh, you were cagey about it – the separate entries are cryptic, but with a reasonable amount of study they lead to only one logical conclusion: your real name is not George Matthews as you would like us to believe, but Edgar Augustus Blunt!'

Jacob interrupted, 'But, Lieutenant, I don't know an Edgar Augustus Blunt. If he exists, shouldn't I know him?'

Anderson shook his head. 'No, it isn't likely you would. His existence was a well-kept secret. Your father never let you know you had a half-brother. But this man is legally your half-brother and I think blood tests will prove it. His mother was a chorus girl in a Broadway musical at the turn of the century. His father was your father. They were never married. Later his mother married a ne'er-do-well actor and threatened to reveal the existence of a son by old Blunt if he did not pay for his support. John Blunt established a living trust which was to continue only as long as the child made no claim to the name of Blunt. In the event of your death, Jacob, this man would inherit your entire estate!'

Anderson turned back to me. 'In a way I'm sorry for you,' he said. 'You must have led a hell of a life as a child. McGillicuddy told me that your mother died soon after giving birth to Frances, her second, and only legitimate, child. You were both raised by her husband and successive nursemaids, your income was stretched to support this man – a broken-down actor – and your half-sister. At one time you even met your half-brother, Jacob. McGillicuddy told me some story about you being fast friends before old Blunt found out about it and separated you. Then your step-father got a contract with a carnival and started touring the country. That is how you and Frances lived for the next five or six years until your step-father died in a drunken brawl.'

Jacob came over to me and stood looking at me. 'Then you must be Pruney,' he said wonderingly. He examined me closely, then turned back to Anderson. 'But he couldn't be, Lieutenant. He doesn't look like him! And Pruney was only a little older than me!'

Anderson riffled the pages of my notebook until he found the photograph of Jacob and his childhood playmate that I had pasted in it. When he found it, he handed the notebook to Sonia, asking, 'How old would you say this person was?'

Sonia looked at the photo for a short while, then handed the book back to Anderson. 'In his teens,' she admitted, 'although he might be almost any age. I never saw such an old face on such a stunted body. But he certainly doesn't look like Dr Matthews!'

'This snapshot was taken fifteen or more years ago,' said Anderson. 'A person can change a great deal in that length of time.'

'Dr Matthews is not Pruney,' Jacob insisted stolidly.

I felt it was about time I came to my own defence. I resented Anderson's absurd claims, particularly since I had reasoned from the same evidence to entirely different conclusions. 'I was born in Indianapolis, Indiana,' I said. 'My father's name was Ernest Matthews and my mother's name was Martha. My name has never been any other. I am in no way related to Jacob, and if you will check the records at the courthouse in Indianapolis they will prove it.'

'You will be given the opportunity to prove it,' said Anderson, 'but I doubt your ability.' He looked searchingly at me. 'I think your name is Blunt, and I know your half-sister's name is Frances Raye. I think you hated this half-sister, just as you hated your mother before her. I think you hated Jacob, too, and felt that all of them stood between you and your rightful inheritance. I think that you had planned for a long time—'

I broke in. 'Do you really want to know who killed Frances Raye, Nan Bulkely and—' my voice broke – 'and now Sara?' I had grown tired of his wrong-headed charges.

'I think you did,' said Anderson.

'Give me a chance to prove you wrong,' I pleaded. 'Give me until tomorrow morning. If I don't have final, irrefutable proof of my own innocence and the murderer's guilt by then, you can do what you think best.'

Anderson studied me for a long moment. I thought he was going to grant my request, but then he shook his head. 'No,' he said, 'once before I took a chance with you, George – and I regretted it. Now I'm placing you under arrest—'

He reached out to take my arm and handcuff me. I hated to do it, but there was no other way out – I stepped forward and hit him hard on the side of the jaw. He fell sprawling on the floor. I ran out the door, vaulted down the stairs to the street. A policeman and a detective – Sommers, dozing as usual – stood on either side of the entrance to the house. I went past them so fast that I was in Anderson's car and had released the clutch – the motor was running – before they knew what I was doing. The car roared down the street in second. I shifted into high as I turned the corner. In rapid succession I heard shouts, the shrilling of police whistles and the windshield shattered as a bullet struck it. But by then I was in the clear – I had turned on to Eighth Street from Fifth Avenue and was racing for Third Avenue. Canal Street and the Bridge . . .

2

I had never driven that recklessly before and I hope I never have to again. I drove through traffic lights, busy intersections – once I narrowly missed colliding with a brewery truck. I ignored the brakes, using them only when the police car began to sway dangerously going around a corner or when a street car blocked my path. I turned on the radio and heard news of my escape being broadcast to all other scout cars. But by the time I reached 5755 Ocean Avenue none of them had found me yet.

I went there because this was the address I had scribbled under the name 'Edgar Augustus Blunt' on the back of the photograph months ago, and also because I had now remembered what I had done that last day of April: I had gone to 5755 Ocean Avenue to confront the murderer. One other time I had visited this address, if by accident, and that was a few nights ago when I had taken a walk in the Coney Island neighbourhood and had stood and laughed at my reflection in the crazy mirror.

Yes, 5755 Ocean Avenue was the address of the Fun House! As I drew up along the kerb in front of it, I noticed that there was a sign pasted over the box-office window that read 'Closed for Repairs'. I paid no attention to this sign but pushed up the latch that barred the flimsy, gaudily streak-painted door and walked inside.

It was pitch dark. I stood still until my eyes became accustomed to the blackness. My heart pounded against my ribs as I saw that the only way to go was along a steep, narrow, twisting passageway. I told myself that this place was just like many amusement concessions I had visited in my childhood at Indianapolis; but my head told me that it differed in one essential: somewhere inside lurked a murderer. I began to climb the tortuous passage.

Soon I could see nothing even when I looked around for the slit of light that marked the door by which I had entered. I felt along the wall as I climbed to find that it was of the roughest plaster and an old nail that obtruded tore at my hands. I kept climbing, higher and higher. Sometimes the floor seemed to drop away from under me – these were the hinged boards meant to give pleasurable scares to amusement-seekers. Then, after I had climbed for about five minutes, the passageway began to steepen. Jets of air blew up my trousers, a thin stream of water spurted into my face. Another time I would have laughed, but instead I climbed grimly upward.

What I expected to find at the top of the passage was a way down into the interior of the Fun House. I remembered only vaguely the time I had been here before; that is, I could remember entering and climbing the same steep ascent. I remember that other things had happened too, horrible things, but what had gone wrong? I stopped and decided to try to collect my thoughts, sort out my memories, so I would be prepared for what would happen next.

From the moment I had struck Anderson and dashed pell-mell for the car until then I had not paused for deliberation. I knew roughly what my plan was, but it had been formed under great pressure of time. Now I could afford a breathing spell. I fumbled in my pocket for a cigarette and a match and in so doing I must have shifted my weight heavily from one foot to another and pressed a movable board for the floor fell out from under me.

I was slipping, sliding, madly scrambling down, down, down. And, at the same time, I heard a shrill laugh that went on and on in a spasm of hysterical merriment!

I slid faster and faster until my body began to scorch through my clothes because of the awkward position I had fallen into and the needless friction it caused. I knew from the way I was falling that I was going down a slide, but it was many seconds before I was thrown forward at last on my hands and knees at its bottom. As I stood up on what was apparently a gently sloping, polished surface, the lights went on dimly. These were only a few dusty bulbs strung haphazardly in odd corners of the cavernous, vaulted structure with its mazes of passages and surprising devices. The slide had deposited me in the centre of a turntable – one of those rides that begins to revolve slowly as you cling to the high centre and spins faster and faster until centrifugal force tears you away and flings you off tangentially. High above me were tier after tier of balconies, partly covered, that ringed the barnlike building. When the Fun House was open, customers entered from the street as I had done, walked along these ascending balconies until they reached the drop-off unexpectedly and fell headfirst down the slide . . . Just as I came to this conclusion, I heard again that laugh.

I looked upwards towards the ceiling and saw a

catwalk high in the rafters – there, partly in shadow, his back turned to a giant switchboard, I saw my adversary – Eustace.

He was dressed in the same absurd velvet jacket, tattersall waistcoat and ridiculous mauve broadcloth trousers as he had been the first day I saw him. He looked down at me and laughed again.

I had been a fool. Now I remembered fully my previous experience in this same Fun House not more than three months before. Then, too, I had tracked him here, caught him, only to find myself caught, a helpless prisoner. And I remembered how he had freely admitted his crimes at that time, bragging about them to me. He had tried to kill me then and he had failed. Now it was my turn.

'Well, Doctor, shall we try it again?' As Eustace leaned down from his platform high above me, he flicked a switch and the turntable I was on began to revolve very slowly. 'You have regained your memory, haven't you? You have rediscovered your theory that I am the murderer!'

'Yes,' I said. 'Aren't you?'

Eustace leaned far over the guard rail of the high platform. 'Why ask me, Doctor? Why don't you tell me as you did once before? You had it all figured out. My name was not Felix Mather, not even Eustace, but Edgar Augustus Blunt, old John Blunt's unacknowledged son. You even told me why I killed Frances. You said I hated her because she was my mother's daughter and that I hated my mother because she bore me. You said that who I really hated, and could do nothing about my hate because he was dead, was my father. John Blunt. You even had a name for my motivation – you called it "illicit transference". You said my natural love for my mother had been thwarted when I was a child by my father and

209

had turned into an unnatural obsession against Frances and Jacob, my half-sister and half-brother.'

'And I was right!' I exclaimed. Eustace leaned over the rail until he seemed to be dangling by his hand which clung to a lever on the wall behind – actually a slim guard rail protected him.

'Yes,' he cried, 'you were right. Of course, I hated them. I hate every one of you long-legged, straight-bodied, huge, overbearing people. But Jacob and Frances I hated particularly. One of them had my father, the other shared my mother. Yet neither of them was like me. Why? I've asked myself that question a hundred thousand times. My father did not reject me because my mother was not married to him. No, he rejected me because my face and body revolted him, because he could not stand the sight of me!

'Why should Jacob be straight, handsome, tall, while I was a dwarf? Why should Frances be beautiful, while I was loathsome and frightening? Why should I be content with a trust fund and the name Mather when a great fortune was Jacob's? Mather! I hate that name! It was my mother's name before she married Raye. When I lived with him and Frances after my mother's death – when we travelled back and forth across the country with a carnival – even then I was different. Raye lived off my money and called himself my guardian. That brat of his, that pig-tailed Frances, wouldn't even play with me! She called me Pruney. It was then, years and years ago, that I made up my mind to kill her eventually. Then one year we came to New York . . .'

'Where you used to play in Central Park. Where you met Jacob and the two of you became good friends. Why should you hate him now?'

'Jacob!' the dwarf screamed wrathfully. 'All he has is mine rightfully!' He was nearly hysterical, maniacally angry. He yelled some incoherent sentences I could not understand. Then he paused and went on more quietly. 'Jacob was my brother at one time. Really my brother. Those were the days when we played together in Central Park. I knew who he was because my mother had showed me a picture of him she had clipped from the papers before she died. He did not know who I was, yet he accepted me, liked me, was my friend. But that did not last. One day my father came and found him with me in the Park, took him away. He was never allowed to play with me again after that. And I grew to hate him, too!' His voice had risen shrilly again.

'You travelled with the carnival some more after that,' I said. 'When you came of age, what did you do with your income?'

'I bought this place for my amusement,' he shouted down at me. 'I run the controls, see?' He pressed a lever and the turntable I was on began to revolve faster. 'Every summer I sit up here, high above everyone else, looking down at all the fools who come in here, playing tricks on them. I throw the switches, press the buttons. I blow up the girls' skirts, tilt the floors, cause farting noises to sound, scare them, bedevil them, make them even more ridiculous than they seem to think I am . . .'

'When I came here in April, you admitted that you killed Raye,' I shouted up at him. 'You killed her in such a way that the police were bound to think Jacob did it – or that was the way your plan should have worked. You hired midgets from a side-show to help you persuade Jacob to do insane things, dressed them up in queer suits and provided them with money. Jacob fell in with your plan, but he acted intelligently twice. He came to see me and he refused to deliver the percheron. So when you murdered Raye, there was no one to blunder into her apartment afterwards.'

'That's right as far as it goes,' said Eustace. 'I hired Tony to drive the truck that carried Jacob and the percheron to Raye's apartment. But I did not know that Jacob would get wary and refuse to ring her doorbell. I planned to have him discover her body, phone for the police and tell them his crazy story. If he didn't get convicted of first degree murder for that they would certainly declare him criminally insane and either way I would get his fortune.

'But he told you too much for my good. And, while I was inside Raye's apartment, he decided not to go through with the delivery of the horse. I had knifed Raye and made my escape through the dumbwaiter – I got out at an empty apartment and waited in the hall until the coast was clear – when a scout car frightened Tony, the driver of the truck, just as he was delivering the horse. Caught in the act he, stupidly, told the story Jacob was supposed to tell.'

The turntable was spinning faster and faster and I was growing dizzy. But I knew I must keep Eustace talking. I remembered what had happened before, how I had tried to escape by one of the exits and he had pushed a lever that brought a crushing weight down on me . . .

'So then you sent Nan down to Police Headquarters to bail Tony out and to try to get hold of me. You wanted to get me to tell you Jacob's whereabouts. After I was foolish enough to allow Tony to be released into my custody, Nan pushed me into the train and searched my pockets for the photograph of you that Jacob must have told you he had given to me. She didn't find it because it was in my other suit hanging in my closet in my house. So Nan and Tony took me to Nan's apartment and you conceived of the brilliant idea of having a quack doctor ïock treatments to me to make me tell you ïidn't know: where Jacob was.'

'I'll never believe that you didn't know,' Eustace said. 'I still think you know where he is.'

'You mean you haven't found him yet. But why are you still looking for him?'

'And you,' said Eustace. 'Both of you know too much about what I've done. That's why I killed Nan this morning. And that's why I killed your wife this afternoon. I came into the hallway of your apartment house and saw the door open. I crept inside and threw a knife into her back from a distance of six feet. It was a perfect shot – she didn't make a sound.'

I hated him. His small figure made a great swinging shadow that whirled and danced in ellipses and circles as I revolved around it. I had to crane my head to see him, high on his tiny catwalk, and this accentuated my dizziness and made the pit of my stomach reel.

'Why didn't you kill me then?' I asked.

'I wanted to talk to you. I knew you would find me again, and I wanted you, of all people, to know my plan. And then you could tell me where Jacob is.'

'Yes,' I said. 'I can tell you that. But first you must answer some questions for me. Do you agree?'

He bobbed his head in assent. I had an idea. It was dangerous, but that did not matter. If it did not work, I would die anyway – only, perhaps, a little sooner. 'One thing I want to know,' I asked, 'is how you managed to get Nan Bulkely to help you with your plan?'

'I gave her presents at first. Then I promised her the lead in *Nevada!* – although she did not know I planned to grant that promise by killing Raye – and a Central Park apartment. Until Raye was murdered she thought the things I was doing were all parts of a complicated practical joke I wanted to play on a friend. After that she was afraid to do other than what I told her for she knew I would kill her.'

I was right when I guessed that Nan had been as much a prisoner as myself, and that she had been acting against her own will. 'Another thing I want to know,' I said, 'is why you had Nan get you percherons to tie to the lamppost when you committed a crime?'

Eustace threw back his head and cackled. This time his laughter was higher and shriller than before, an especially grisly sound to hear. 'I like percherons,' he said. 'They're my trademark. My way of setting a seal on my work – they're so big and powerful, just the opposite of me.'

'Were you the one who called Nan last night?' I asked.

'Yes,' he said. 'That was after I had Nan rent another percheron. I told her I wanted it for you and that I would telephone her and tell her where to have it delivered. But when I phoned she told me she was through. Then I knew I had to kill her. I trailed Jacob and her to the Village, waited until they left the night club and the park and were walking a deserted street. Then I shot her and went to get the percheron which I had had delivered in a truck a block or so away.'

'Why didn't you kill Jacob then?' I asked.

'I planned to, but just as I was taking aim I heard somebody open a window in the house behind me. I might have had a witness if I had shot again. So I beat it and threw away the gun. If I had used knives it might have been different. I'm good with knives, and knives are even quieter than a silenced gun. I learned to throw them at the carnival. See?' And as he spoke, his figure lunged and a long hunting knife buried itself in the wood of the turn-table inches from my head. I knew then that I had only seconds to wait. I clambered to my knees, clutching desperately for handholds on the smooth wood as the machine whirled faster and faster.

214

'One more question, Eustace,' I cried up at him. 'What did you do with me after you tried to kill me here in this place last spring and what did you do with Tony's body after the taxi accident?'

'I put a fake Social Security Card in your pocket after frisking your identification,' he said, 'and hired a couple of friends of mine – good boys who work around here – to dump you along the Bowery. I thought you were dead at the time or I wouldn't have let you go. As for Tony, he died in Nan's apartment after the taxi accident. We put your clothes on him and threw him in the river. It was the safest place for him.'

He was silent. I could see that he was leaning far over the guard railing, peering down at me, his hand on the lever. The turntable was going so rapidly now that I knew I could not hold on much longer. I saw him raise his small hand, saw the gleam of a disproportionately large knife in it . . .

'You told me that you would tell me where Jacob is now. I've got to find him. As long as he lives I shall not be free. This morning, if I had had this, I would have killed him. Now, quickly, tell me where he is!'

I stood up dizzily, balancing precariously on the very centre of the turntable. I knew I made a better target like that and also that I would soon be thrown off. But if this came off I would have to be as dramatic as I could . . .

'Right behind you, Pruney!' I cried. 'Look, Jacob is right there behind you!'

It worked. I don't know whether it was the old taunt, the sound of the ancient ridicule that startled him, or whether he so ardently desired to see Jacob that he did not think. But he tried to face about instantly and, delicately balanced on the guard rail as he was, he wrenched his hand free from the controls, swayed sickeningly and fell off the catwalk. He gave one whistling cry before he struck the floor thirty feet below. He must have died instantly. Unhappily, in death his stunted body and absurdly wrinkled face looked as much a caricature of human features as they had in life.

But I was not pitying Eustace then. I maintained my balance for one moment more, time enough to see Lieutenant Anderson and one of his men detach themselves from the darkness of a balcony and come clattering down a stairway to the ground floor – and to realize that they had been part of the greater shadow long enough to have heard every word of Eustace's confession.

Then I just let go and swung off into space.